UNfatally DEAD:
to thaw or not to thaw?

by Wayne Edmiston

Adapted from a screenplay by the same title and
cowritten with former creative partners ©1986

WEDMISTON
WED∞
PUBLISHING

Copyright © 2018 Wayne Edmiston for WEDmiston Publishing

Typeset in Adobe Garamond, Gabriola, and Native by Claudia Previn Creative, San Diego, CA
Cover designer: Krista Lynn, Krystallyn Designs, CA

ISBN-13: ISBN 978-0-9993698-0-7

Printed in the United States of America

Publisher's Cataloging-In-Publication Data
(Prepared by The Donohue Group, Inc.)
Names: Edmiston, Wayne.
Title: Unfatally dead : to thaw or not to thaw? / by Wayne Edmiston.
Description: [Arroyo Grande, California] : WEDmiston Publishing, [2018]
    | "Adapted from a screenplay by the same title and cowritten with
    former creative partners ©1986."
Identifiers: ISBN 9780999369807 (print) | ISBN 9780999369814 (ebook)
Subjects: LCSH: Disney, Walt, 1901-1966--Fiction. | Twain, Mark,
    1835-1910--Fiction. | Cryonics--Fiction. | Time travel--Fiction.
    | World history--Fiction. | LCGFT: Humorous fiction. | Science
    fiction. | Historical fiction. | Fantasy fiction. | BISAC: YOUNG
    ADULT FICTION / Time Travel. | FICTION / Fantasy / Historical.
    | FICTION / Science Fiction / Action & Adventure. | HISTORY /
    Modern / 20th Century. | FICTION / General.
Classification: LCC PS3605.D559 U54 2018 (print) | LCC PS3605.D559
    (ebook) | DDC 813/.6--dc23

Acknowledgments

Every aspect of bringing this tale to light has been a labor of love. The story first took form through my late wife, Sherry Plaster Edmiston (1944–1989), and lay dormant for some years. Inspiration came like a flame a couple of years ago, flickered, then flared into an urge, igniting it into another incarnation—first a screenplay, and now a book.

My love of these last 25 years has been with me every step of the way. Thank you, Jacque. Your patience, understanding nature, and all-power-full love keeps me warm day and night.

My editor, Claudia Previn Stasny, has kept me on my toes. She has been a diligent, unrelenting guide to make this book possible.

To my dear friends Jacqueline Chohan and Rajinder Khokhar, I thank you for your insights, thoughtfulness, and dedication to writing; you have helped me immensely.

To the Los Angeles and Hollywood Screenplay contests, thank you for permitting the screenplay to be an official finalist.

To WILDsound Writing Festival, thank you for your generous review and feedback. The log line on You Tube looks great, not to mention your estimable comments. You have helped more than you could possibly know—hence the creation of this book.

To the Atascadero Writers Group, thank you for taking the time to read and discuss more than one of my projects. This is what writing is all about, cooperative ventures, mutual respect, and admiration of the written word.

Most of all thank you, kind reader. I trust you will enjoy what comes next.

Contents

Prologue

THE handsome, snappily dressed little rodent with oversized ears scampered as fast as his little legs could carry him, determinedly chasing after an ambulance as it navigated a maze of streets in the Los Angeles suburbs.

It had rained ferociously throughout that cold December day, and he had to scurry and leap around myriad storm-tossed obstacles, both man-made and natural. He risked drowning at least three different times during the chase when water splashed over him from passing cars and trucks—and an unswerving bicyclist who missed him by mere inches and created a wave from the gutter that inundated him and left him sputtering for breath.

Thinking the worst was over, suddenly he heard a loud rending noise—painful to his sensitive ears. The sound was almost deafening. The biggest surprise, however, was the huge tree limb that slammed down in front of him. He blinked in amazement that it had missed him. Given his diminutive size, any limb posed potential disaster.

Chilled to the bone, buffeted by driving wind and rain, he paused to consider his options: the only way forward was either over or under it. And because the large limb was already half floating, over seemed the most likely choice.

He took a deep breath, gathered his strength and jumped as high up as he could, grasped two branches and propelled his little body over this latest obstacle … only to land headfirst in a child's discarded wooden boat floating in the storm water. The rain-swollen gutters were now near floodwater levels, at least for a creature his size.

Not knowing what could possibly be next, he squeezed his eyes shut and prayed, "Squeak, squeak!" and held on for dear life. The churning current tossed him about—a helpless rodent in a discarded boat—faster and faster the current pushed and swirled, hurtling him along with it.

Then he saw what was ahead: a huge storm drain!

He had mere moments to decide whether to go down with the ship or abandon it. At the final second, he found out a desperate leap of faith was all he needed. He landed on solid ground and scampered about, relieved and confused and trying his utmost to regain his bearings.

Between these mishaps and the little tyke's short legs, he had not kept pace with the ambulance, but his heightened hearing, attuned to the vehicle's sounds as it churned ahead without him, put him on the right track. He forged ahead, even more determined than before. Every so often he stopped to catch his breath, shake off the water, and listen for the next direction to take. By now we're wondering, where is he going and who or what is he following?

He arrived at last next to the ambulance that had parked near the stairs to a building where he knew his creator and father was. He labored for breath and, cold and wet from his headlong pursuit, he shivered, shook, and gasped—as any near–40-year-old mouse certainly would—especially when a normal life span is no more than a year or so.

This was no ordinary mouse!

He hopped up the three steps and stood transfixed, intently listening to sounds on the other side of the massive doorway that now separated him from his goal. Incoherent little squeaks escaped his trembling mouth, and his whiskers twitched back and forth as his mouth moved. What was the rodent saying?

Let's listen in, shall we?

"Walt, are you there? It's me, Mickey, your son! I've known you all my life and now you're leaving me behind to face the unknown. We've worked together for nearly four decades and there's so much more to do! I cannot do it without you."

Mickey choked back huge tears of frustration and anguish and pleaded, "Papa, don't go just yet! Walt, are you there, can you hear me? What will Minnie and I do without you? How can we survive? Remember our first venture together? You showed me piloting a steamboat on the Mississippi River, and you even changed my name from Mortimer to Steamboat Willie for that movie."

He heard footsteps approaching the other side of the door. The white-uniformed men nearly stepped on Mickey as they came through, and he scampered aside to avoid being trampled. They pushed a now-empty gurney where he'd seen them place his father and creator and hurry from the secure, private quarters and hidden facility at a place that bore his name: Disneyland.

As they whisked by, Mickey heard the ambulance men talking about his master.

The first man said, "He looked more sorry-full than ever, pitiful really. I wonder if these folks will be able to do what they have been contracted to do."

The second man responded, "I dunno, it hasn't been done before, as far as I know. I'd say his chances are between slim and none, but I'm not the one in the driver's seat."

"Well, hardly anyone has an imagination like his, so I figure there must be a better-than-nothing chance that somewhere, somehow, he will come back. God only knows when or if!"

"Right you are. Say, what about stopping at our favorite burger joint? I'm famished!"

"Good idea. If we get another call as urgent as this one, I'm gonna need some refueling vittles-wise."

The little mouse hadn't eaten either—for how long? He couldn't remember the last time he'd had a bit of cheese, a morsel of any kind, and his little stomach growled a reminder. He sniffed the air for food but was disappointed—no such luck.

Mickey Mouse decided he would not go anywhere until he could see his master and creator for one last and final time. "Intellectual property rights be hanged," he planned to say. "Please take me with you."

....

What was happening on the other side of the doorway that separated our famous little friend and companion from Walt Disney?

∞

CHAPTER *1*

The Journey Begins

INSIDE the building, a mere whisper of life remained in Walter Elias Disney. His body was surrounded by cryoprotectant containers, tanks, cryostats, tubes and transfer systems, the best 1960s technology available.

The look and smell of the entire facility were sanitary down to the last detail. Safety regulations warned strict enforcement on a massive bulletin board in the entry lobby.

In a large lab beyond, the cryonics team hovered, busily making final equipment checks while the medical team carefully and efficiently monitored their patient, the sacred founder of Imagineering entertainment. Every action was critical. Everyone's awareness was at its height. Several medical professionals vigorously verified and documented every second until Disney's impending cardiac arrest.

Minutes seemed to crawl by, the waiting was so intense. Outside, the storm blustered and wailed as if it might clamor through the walls.

The facility's intentionally soothing ambient music was turned off, in deference to who was being preserved. Not a sound came from the loudspeaker system on this dreary, unsettled afternoon.

As Disney's transitional moment drew near, the teams' work escalated. Each member was determined to prevent any possible premature decomposition of the one and only original "Imagineer." Several technicians were trembling slightly, reverently muttering about the man who had brought so much joy to the entire world.

Technician Jimmy Doolittle broke the silence and exclaimed with a gasp, "Holy cow! I grew up with the Mouseketeers and the Mickey Mouse Club … and here I am helping to launch Disney himself into the stratosphere of cryonic suspension. Wait till I tell my kids!"

Supervisor Dr. Andy Susskind, extremely tired from a long, tedious, all-night shift, tersely instructed, "On the contrary. Remember, this must be kept secret from all sources, and I mean all of them. You've sworn allegiance to this facility and I expect you to honor the agreement you signed." He added, resigned to the possibility, "or have you forgotten so soon?"

"You're right," Doolittle said, chastened. "I got caught up in the moment because of who this is. These tight lips are sealed and will open none too soon, if ever."

"Good, see that you mean it. I guess I don't need to remind you about our confidentiality agreements, then?"

"No, sir."

Disney's vital-signs monitor suddenly sounded a warning.

Susskind exclaimed, "Flat line! It is time. Once every process is complete, we'll continuously monitor Disney's body under the strictest security conditions and protocols. Let's get to it!"

All hands then functioned swiftly and efficiently, as if they embodied a single unit of consciousness, each person at peak attention. Every process went as planned; the countless, necessary drills paid off: no interruptions, no missteps, and definitely no mistakes.

Only close family members—Lillian his wife, daughter Diane, and his brother Roy—gathered around Disney's bed. Teary-eyed Roy stood at Walt's feet. Unconsciously he sought to rub them as he had done so many times in the past, because his little brother had had chronically cold feet. In mid-reach, he stopped short and, with a huge lump in his throat, sadly muttered, "I guess you won't be needing me to rub them any longer..." Legal representatives from Crockett, Poppins, and Hood stood at a respectful distance, ready to ensure powers smoothly transferred to the appropriate parties.

The initial flurry of medical activity subsided and, their tasks complete, the teams stepped back to make room for Disney's family and friends to bid him farewell ... for now.

The Reverend Dr. Fenwicke Holmes, pristinely dressed, moved gently and authoritatively to the front of the gathered group and intoned, "We are here in the presence of and with the Creator. We stand witness to a future in which humankind can be free of terminal ailments. Our timeless, ageless friend has endured much pain and suffering. He is now being placed in the care of holy advanced technologies, the result of collective efforts by superior forward thinkers."

He paused and breathed deeply before continuing, "Just a few days ago I spoke with him. He said to me: 'Bring me back, safe, well, and of ... sound mind.'

"We now place his request into the Law of Mind, trusting it will be acted upon with the knowledge that all things are possible in the embracing arms of the God of our understanding. Together let us know this event, whose beginnings we witness today, happens in the right time, the right conditions prevail, and the subsequent outcome is in perfect right, divine order. Amen and so it is."

Hovering at a respectful distance, several technicians, including the standby and transport teams, stood poised and ready for the ensuing rigorous 170 hours of cryopreservation.

Dr. James Gold, CEO of the cryonics organization, gratefully acknowledged his team's efficiency and effectiveness and continued, "All systems are a go. Begin the transfer, let's make history."

∞

CHAPTER *2*

Heaven

A PLACE known to all who have passed into the wild blue yonder, Heaven's Creative Department is headed up by Walt Disney himself. Pink and yellow clouds billow around his workstation. He peers intently through a special pair of goggles plugged into an Infinite Capability Viewer. He fiddles with several settings on a console and keyboard, his attention wholly focused on the view.

Angel Gabriel approaches deferentially, intending not to intrude on the creative process. He is a tall, extraordinarily distinguished-looking gentleman dressed in a long shimmering robe that pulses strobe-lights within its folds. He appears to be deeply troubled as he carefully, thoughtfully walks toward Disney; he stands nearby, still searching for words to open a conversation.

He decides, takes a deep breath, and softly touches Disney's arm. "Excuse me, Walt, an urgent matter. We must talk privately right away. Come to the main office ASAP."

As if he hasn't heard the angel, Disney murmurs, "Sure, Gabe. I'll be there soon."

Gabriel urges intensely, "Not later, Walt. We need to talk now, right now!"

Still engrossed, Disney does not respond to Gabriel's insistent tone. He is busily making large sweeps in the air with his arm, creating cartoons that magically appear then fade from view as he raptly stares into the viewer. He explains, "I'm watching this young girl ... from Livingston, California. Here, look through the viewer." He offers the goggles to Gabriel, "See her?"

Gabriel suppresses his agitation and accedes to Disney. He takes the goggles and looks with genuine interest and compassion, saying nothing.

....

The viewer shows a little eight-year-old girl with deep-set worried brown eyes and a pair of perfectly braided pigtails. She is in a 1950s treatment

9

room—not a school principal's office as we might have expected, but in an optometrist's office, Dr. Musgrave from Turlock, California.

Her anxious mother asks, "Are you OK, honey?" Her daughter nods a cautious yes; she is a bit unnerved by the prospect of someone looking into her eyes to identify what is wrong with her eyesight. "It won't be too much longer, then you can go back to where you need to."

Trailed by a nurse, the doctor walks in, a kind smile for them both, and says to the girl, "Well, Ms. Sherry, let's see what's in there. Open your eyes wide."

Her dilated eyes seemed even larger on her face, and she holds her breath in concentration. "Hold them just like that while I take a look-see." He held up a small lens first to one eye, then the other, pausing briefly before speaking a few sentences that make no sense to anyone except the nurse taking notes. "Got it. OK, Sherry, you can relax."

She had been remarkably patient, but the girl's unease took over and she blurts, "Why don't my eyes work right?"

"Say, you really are a curiosity, aren't you? Your problem is because one eye sees one way and the other another, and one of them tilts, too."

Little Sherry interjects, "I coulda told you that. Can you make me see better?"

The good doctor pats her on her head and turns to the mother, "Your daughter is so precocious! We have just the machine to help her. It came in last week from a special benefactor who incidentally has a little girl nearly Sherry's age with the same problem. He looked for some specific equipment, found it and donated it to our facility, because he hopes to help others see better. With the help of the machine and special eye exercises, she will."

Relieved and excited at the prospect, the mother exclaimed, "That is so wonderful! You must thank the benefactor from our family. We are grateful for his interest in helping not only his daughter, but others with similar eye problems. When do you want us to come back?"

Dr. Musgrave instructed the nurse over his shoulder, "Make an appointment for our special customer for next week and at two-week intervals afterward, and give her the specific eye exercises to do between visits. We'll check her eyes every other month to assess her progress."

"Yes, doctor." She leaves the room with Sherry's file in hand.

The good doctor said, "Mrs. Plaster, your little girl here has a very strong personality and knows what she wants. That's a good thing! I'll do my best to see she gets what she needs."

"Thank you Dr. Musgrave. Yes, she has a decidedly strong personality, and not being able to see as others do is holding her back."

You needn't worry about that any longer. I've had good results already. It will be like a walk in the park."

Little Ms. Sherry interrupts, "Oh goodie, I like to take walks in the park with my doggie, Penny. It's gonna be fun, I think." She hops off the chair, obviously more than ready to get going with everything. "I think I like this man, and the special benny factor. Momma, what's a benny factor?"

"Honey, a ben-eh-factor is someone who gives a valuable gift without any strings attached—not a benny factor. Benny's a comedian on Sunday nights, remember? I know how much you love it when there is a blooper on live television, right?"

"Oh yes I do. Can we go now, I'm hungry!" Little Sherry Plaster is obviously ready to leave.

At the front counter, appointments made, the mother pauses, worried that the treatments will be expensive, even though she is willing to do what is necessary for her daughter. "We don't have a lot of money on hand. May we make weekly payments? My husband is a union painter and he gets paid on Fridays, unless they go out on strike."

The nurse reassures the mom, her voice curiously melodic, "That's not necessary Mrs. Plaster. This benefactor is taking care of all the costs for anyone who needs this specialized treatment. That is his gift for one in need to see rightly."

"Oh my goodness!" Mrs. Plaster is taken aback. "Please tell him how much we appreciate his generosity. Someday, somehow, we'll be able to repay him. This is our sacred promise."

"No need, ma'am. It is his great pleasure to give this gift."

While walking out of the office, Sherry declares to her mother, "I will see better and when I do I'll do something special for him mama, I promise. I'll make him a special picture of happy flowers or something, OK?"

"Yes, that would be a nice present for the man, honey, you do that. Now, since you said you were hungry, what about a toasted cheese sandwich, celery sticks, and maybe some chocolate milk?"

Sherry's eyes dance about as she sees the favorite meal in her mind's eye, "Oh yes please!"

Later, home from school, Sherry runs eagerly to her bedroom, lifts the lid of her well-worn desk—recently donated by the school and now her very own—pulls out a blank sheet of paper and begins drawing and humming. A big grin lights her face and determination shows in her eyes.

....

Walt explains to Gabriel, "She's been having a pretty rough time. She believes she's a misfit because all she wants to do is draw cartoons. See those flowers she's drawn! They have smiles on them! I did that long ago."

Gabriel nods in silent agreement. Disney presses further, "She's been catching grief from her friends and teacher because she's different, doesn't fit the mold. I fear she may want to run away from home. I must find a way to influence her and show the right people her talent." He sweeps his arms through the air and large flowers with smiles on their faces smile and wink at him, then fade.

"I understand how important that is to you," Gabriel's voice is strained, "but we have something more urgent to address immediately. It simply can't wait."

Disney is surprised. He was so intent on watching the little girl he was oblivious until this moment. The hair stands up on the back of his neck and he feels suddenly anxious.

Gabriel's tone is insistent, "You started something before you came here. And now a decision must be made. Time is of the essence. There is no other way to handle this. It must be done, Walt. Come with me!"

Disney feels both perplexed and apprehensive as Gabriel glides away without another word and disappears into a big ornate elevator, visible across the picturesque veranda. The sign above it reads, EXECUTIVE EXPRESS.

He follows reluctantly, and waits for the GENERAL STAFF elevator, not knowing the reason for all this attention focused on him and not the little girl he was so raptly interested in. As the doors slide open, he takes a deep breath and enters. "Well, here goes nothing, I hope."

One hand in his pocket, he presses the big green UP button and looks to the open sky. The sun is glorious and shines in splendor, warming, comforting. The elevator rises three levels and glides to a full stop. The doors automatically slide open and a melodious disembodied voice announces, "We trust you had a nice trip. Have a great day, wherever you are is perfectly perfect."

A long hallway with many doors on either side leads to the easily identified luminous, pearlescent double doors of Heaven's Main Office. When Disney reaches them, the doors open and slide into the wall; harp strings announce him.

Inside, brilliant white "walls" shimmer and golden accessories glint and shine. Several "ponds" dot the office, containing piles of large, highly polished diamonds and jewels that glow in varying colored hues. Crystals spin in the air and send rainbow flashes everywhere. The plush furniture appears to float without support; the legs are transparent.

We see Gabriel busily studying a large, golden book. The title identifies it as a minute-by-minute record of Walt Disney's earthly life of 65 years and 10 days,

The Original Imagineer is exceedingly nervous and watches the angel carefully as he approaches. "This reminds me of my grammar school days. I remember feeling this scared when they called me to report to Principal Kanen's office to discuss how disappointed they were with me."

Gabriel doesn't acknowledge Walt's presence, but continues to peer into and leaf through the pages describing Disney's most intimate moments on earth. Not sure why he's here or how to react, Disney stares down and plays with cloud wisps pooling around his feet. He creates a few cartoons by moving his toes in whirling motions.

Then he looks back at the angel and softly clears his throat. "Ahem! I'm here."

No response or eye contact.

Disney studies Gabriel's face and sees an expression that is a mixture of... concern? Pity?

He sighs and says mostly to himself, "Ohhhhh, this is gonna be a biggie...."

At last, Gabriel looks up and motions to a plush, round-backed chair floating near the cloudy floor. Walt obediently perches self-protectively on the edge of it, should flight become important.

Gabriel places the book on a massive, ornately carved crystal desk, looks intently into Walt's face and smiles warmly. "Please relax, my friend. You have done nothing wrong."

"If that's the case, why all the tension? I sense it everywhere."

"We just feel you should have some advance notice and involvement in the decision-making process. If we didn't alert you, you could be most rudely surprised." Gabriel looks back at something on the desk, ignoring Walt's discomfited squirming.

"I'm ready. Anything is better than what not knowing has been doing to my nerves. What are we talking about anyway?"

"Well, Walt, this is a first for us. Quite frankly we don't know what to do about it." Gabriel is not elaborating yet and simply waits for Disney's response.

Frustrated to the point of being rude Disney demands, "Spit it out, man! What the dickens did I do?"

Gabriel peers right into Walt's heart and soul. "Do you remember making a decision right before your death?"

Confused and surprised by the sudden inquisition, "No, I don't think I made any decisions then."

"Au contraire my friend, you did, an important one."

Walt sinks back into the legless plush chair, sighing and looking utterly forlorn, almost whispering, "I was very weak. My mind was clouded by my illness. No. I am certain I made no decision that requires me to be figuratively 'called on the carpet' here. You must be mistaken."

Gabriel leans forward, his hands braced on the desk and gazes intently at his crestfallen friend, "You made an important contract when you were on your deathbed."

"Contract?" Disney shakes his head, "I don't understand."

"Do you not remember asking for cryonics researchers to explain the procedure of freezing your body until your illness was declared medically manageable?"

Disney nods with growing certainty as recognition slowly seeps in, and sits up straighter. "Yes … it seems I might be brought back to life! Sure, now I remember that. I was so intrigued by the concept. That's why I agreed to participate." He recalls another place, another time…

....

He's in the cryonics firm's main office. In his mind's eye, he revisits the document and, after carefully reading the last page in front of his legal team and the cryonics firm, he sees his signature affixed to the page.

The ink is not the disappearing kind.

He looks at it and says with conviction, "OK, I'm ready. What's next?"

....

In a blink, he's back in Heaven's Main Office, no longer confused, but concerned, "Surely this is not the first you've heard of this. It's been done for years."

Gabriel sits on the crystal desk's corner nearest Disney and spreads his arms in a gesture of helplessness. "Yes, people have been frozen before, but so far nobody under my jurisdiction has ever been revived. Should you choose to return; you would be our first. It raises innumerable questions."

Walt stares blankly into Gabriel's face, stunned, unnerved, and experiencing waves of emotions—from absolute excitement to total and unequivocal terror. "Are you telling me my disease has been resolved?"

"Yes … cured, or at least manageably controlled."

"I'm feeling overwhelmed and weak, which feels familiar. Yes, I remember, I felt it once before, the day they told me my illness was terminal and my days few. Why should I feel it in my soul now? This isn't bad news." He doesn't feel reassured.

"Walt, your contract with the cryonics company orders them to thoroughly examine the possibilities for your physical revival every five years after your death. It has now been nearly half a century … and …"

Walt looks away, unfocused, but snaps back at the angel's next words.

"The attempt will begin in less than 24 hours, earth time."

Disney is agitated and asks, aghast, "How can they just do that? Don't you have some control over this?"

"Calm down, please Walt. You have many things to consider, and very little time to reach an informed decision."

Disney doesn't hesitate. "Just tell me No. You have the power."

Gabriel sits and faces him squarely. "I cannot do that. I will not supersede your original decision, and that is final."

Disney is bordering on belligerence, "What if I don't want to go back? I mean, there are rules: once you pass through the great gates you can't just shoot back to earth, contract or no contract. Is this correct or not?"

Gabriel sidesteps a direct answer and explains, "Under these circumstances you aren't bound by those rules. The contract you signed in 1966 is binding. In your own thoughts you were just there a moment ago."

Disney is very uncomfortable and getting angry. He leaps to his feet and demands, "Binding?!? And if I don't comply, can they sue me?"

Gabriel chooses his next words with exceeding care, "I do understand your reaction, Walt. It will be OK either way. Either way, I promise."

Disney feels tense. "I'm accomplishing many times the amount of good for humanity from here at my soul level, much more than I did on earth," he says, considering. "At least that's what I can garner from my observations and enhanced capabilities through the goggles back in my department."

Gabriel asks solemnly, "How do you know that? What might you accomplish when or if you return with the insights you enjoy now?"

Walt registers surprise. He stands straighter, then paces a few steps.

His eyes begin to dance as he reviews the possibilities. "Would I remember what I've been doing as head of Heaven's Creative Department? I must admit, I do wonder what life on earth would be like now. Could I eat a candied apple and enjoy some strong, black coffee once more, maybe even a smoke or two?"

"Yes. You would be present and could enjoy the pastimes a mortal person does. However, don't waste precious time on the sin of gluttony because you will have only a limited time to experience each year while using your own judgment, good or not. And you are no longer mortal, remember, because of your smoking."

"I do have some time to—wait!" Struggling to understand, he asks, "What do you mean I have only a 'limited time'? Are you telling me this return to life on earth isn't permanent?"

Gabriel takes a deep breath before continuing, almost squirming in his glossy high-back winged chair as he gets to the crux of the matter, "Your final choice, be it a return to life or a continuation of your days in Heaven, will be permanent. I am speaking of granting you a limited preview time."

Now obviously delighted, Disney asks, "You have an earth viewer that allows me to preview what my life will be like if they revive me? Wow! Where is it?"

"Better than that. You have been granted special dispensation to walk the earth as a flesh-and-blood mortal."

This stuns him. "You mean ... walk on the streets, in the rain, splashing in the gutters like Gene Kelly did in 'Singing in the Rain'? That kind of stuff? For real?"

"Yes, for real. With some stipulations, of course."

Walt tenses with an "I knew it was too good to be true" expression on his face. He gingerly sits back down to be apprised of the remaining rules.

Gabriel stands up, walks around the desk, and delivers the specifics, "You will have up to one hour maximum per experience. The dates and timing of some of your appearances are predetermined, actual world changing events; others will stream from your own consciousness, determination, and intuition as to where, when, and why they unfold."

"Up to one hour per experience only? What years?"

"Your first adventure is to begin a few years after your mortal death, as I understand it."

"What's the purpose? What can I possibly learn in a mere hour?"

"You may interact in ways that touch peoples' soul essence. What happens then is up to that person to do what is appropriate for them. You, Walter Elias Disney, are a visionary, an emissary of sorts, not a missionary nor to be confused as one. Other than finding out what impact you may have had on various and sundry people's lives, you are in complete control of the knowledge you gather or dismiss. We hope to counsel you to reach the right decisions, but you are the sole person in charge of the value of your preview time"—and under his breath, "mostly"—"like it or not."

Disney is floored. "God only knows what shape my company's in today, and I don't want my future actions to tarnish it."

Gabriel's response is full of tenderness, "You'll find out soon enough, Walt."

"But what if someone recognizes me? Is that some kind of test that poses both a problem and an opportunity? I don't know if I could handle it, especially if I were to be recognized after nearly 50 years."

Gabriel smiles knowingly and holds a mirror in front of Walt's face.

Disney looks shocked. "This is supposed to be me? I never ever looked like this, not even at a distance, or close up."

Gabriel laughs at the absurdity, "Oh, the magic of Heaven at work! How you appear now is a compilation of everything your soul has experienced since you arrived here. As your compassion grows, it shows in your face, although your voice remains the same. See how kind your face is now?"

Disney is both perplexed and fascinated at the prospect. "Hmmm, I guess so."

"Your essence will touch many hearts and everyone you meet. This is who they will see."

. . . .

Toward the end of this explanation, a white-haired man in his late 60s, chewing on an unlit cigar, ambles lamely into the office through a different set of doors. He is the exact image of every photograph of Samuel Clemens, aka Mark Twain, taken during the author's later years: rumpled white suit, unkempt and bushy hair. He comments amiably, "That's a lot of hooey."

Gabriel and Disney turn toward him—he has shattered the intensity of the moment—they welcome their witty companion.

Clemens demands, "If that's a true statement and your image changes when you get up here, how is it that I'm not changed one little stitch?" He snatches the mirror and makes faces into it.

Gabriel is put off by the challenge but says politely, "Sometimes change can be very, very slow to show up, but fear not, it will happen given enough time, Sam."

Disney looks his friend and earthly mentor up and down, "How else would the beloved authoritative writer, author, and speaker look? I personally get a lot of assurance, knowing he is immediately recognizable."

Clemens issues a mock warning, "Don't you realize where you two gents are? There're mighty fierce penalties for slingin' that sort of stuff around."

Gabriel and Disney burst into wide smiles and the tension evaporates.

Sam asks slyly, "Did I intrude on something secretive … I hope?"

Gabriel is quick to answer, "Yes, this is a private and urgent conversation, Sam, so we must ask you to excuse us."

"Why-y-y? What'd he do?" He shifts from one foot to another, looks at Disney attentively, and asks, "What'd you do, Walt?"

"Please, Sam, this is important."

"Okay, but I'm bored, bored, bored! Any suggestions for me, maybe something exciting to do?" He shakes his head, shrugs his shoulders. "They won't give me wings," pointing above his head, "and my halo fell off long ago. There's nothing fun left to do here."

Gabriel eyes sparkle with sudden excitement. "Wait a minute, I have an idea! Take Sam Clemens with you, Walt."

Both Disney and Clemens look shocked, then a delighted grin blooms across Disney's face. He likes the idea.

Gabriel is amused. "You'll have someone to converse with, and it'll be a learning experience for Sam."

He cuts his eyes upward and says, almost to himself, "I hope I can get approval for this," and walks to one of the crystals swirling in the air. He touches it gently. The room turns pink as a very deep voice vibrates through the air.

The heavenly voice of God booms out, rich, deep, and authoritative, "Ye-e-e-es-s-s??"

Gabriel is surprisingly meek, "Sir, I would like to ask for special dispensation for Samuel Clemens to accompany Walt Disney back to 1968 and travel together until 2016."

"For what purpose?"

"To assist with Disney's impending decision. It will also be a golden opportunity for Sam to gain heavenly points toward his growth scope."

The deep, majestic voice chuckles, "Yes-s, he is severely deficient in that department, and extraordinarily high in the demerit department."

Clemens crosses his arms in a huff. He traverses to the larger jeweled pond and begins to sift through the diamonds, pretending to deliberately ignore being the object of discussion. He tucks a brilliant jewel—the size of a pocket watch—into his jacket.

Gabriel is wary about whether his idea will be approved, but asks, "Then it's agreed? Shall Sam and Walt go together to review the last half century of earth changes?"

The silence seems to stretch for eons. Then, "Yes, on one condition."

The three wait, poised for what's next. "A new soul is apprenticing with the Akashic Records Department. She shall accompany your travelers to be certain they do not change, alter, modify, vary, or amend any past events."

Clemens looks around and shakes his head furiously from side to side.

The masterful voice booms, "You have a problem with this, Sam?

He protests, pulling at his shirt collar as if it were overly starched, and staunchly refuses, saying, "I'm not gonna take any part in breaking in a new soul. They're pitifully naïve—and she is a woman! No, I'm not gonna do it!"

Gabriel nods briefly, understanding, then raises his arms upward in invitation.

A swing descends dramatically, ethereal music and colors cascade from above. A lavender mist arrives and swirls around the swing. A soft, unemotional female voice greets the three shyly. "My name Eepia. Eepia really will do a good job for you."

She has a stilted speech pattern indicating she is not yet at ease with their language or jargon. Disney interjects, gallantly, "Forgive me, Eepia. I've never met a new soul before. I seem to be having a problem seeing your face."

Clemens is irritated. "Consarn it Walt, they have no faces, they are that new. They walk around askin' everybody, 'What's that?' and 'How come yer doing that?' They will send you round the bend if ya spend much time with them."

Gabriel reiterates emphatically, "Do you remember, Walt, I said that everything you do shows up as character on your face? She has not had a chance to become visible because she is brand new. With time, Eepia will take on her own traits. Have you not noticed Sam's still the same?"

Disney disregards this line of questioning, because he's remembered what he was doing before coming to the office and needs an answer. "Before we go back in time, I really want to help that little cartoonist I was observing earlier."

"Don't worry Walt, she'll be just fine. Your situation is much more urgent. The three of you are to leave immediately."

Clemens shakes his head, walks to another pond, picks up a large diamond, exhales sharply on it and polishes it on his coat. Gabriel glides over, puts his hands on Clemens' shoulders and turns him back around with minimal effort. "Samuel, you will be accompanying Walt and Eepia. You, too, will be a solid projection, enabling you to communicate openly with the people you will encounter."

Clemens is adamant, remains stubborn, "Hold on … I didn't agree to any of this."

Gabriel ignores Sam's retort and instructs them, "You'll arrive at random times and places for up to one hour in any given year, based mostly on Walt's thoughts, desires, intentions, and particular 'imagineering' style. You'll visit different events in the history of the last half century or so of earth years."

Clemens puffs out his chest, "Don't I get any say about this?"

Gabriel glares into Clemens' eyes, challenging him, "Ahem, you don't want to participate?"

"Why no, I didn't say that, no siree! I just feel like a piece of bloody rare steak arriving on a restaurant plate. I have no say in my immediate fate and I don't like it."

Gabriel pats Clemens on his back to comfort him. "I'm sorry Sam, this inordinate amount of pressure must be difficult for you, but we are facing a deadline. When you finish your experience in any year, you will be transported quickly and immediately to another historical time frame, depending on what Walt has been thinking about, and eventually meet back here with me."

Clemens chews defiantly on the still unlit cigar. "No!"

Gabriel ignores this interjection and turns to Disney. "Once back here, we'll visit your current physical body. Then you will decide whether to return to earth life in 2016, or decide to stay here with us, doing what you do best for the rest of eternity."

Clemens, defiant, protests, "Why was I never given a chance to go back to my past? I left behind a few people and some outstanding loans I'd like more than a little bit to spend time enjoying their rewards of. Also, I'd like to help reseed a few acres in Nevada I accidentally burned up."

Gabriel is adamant, "Not possible, my friend. You see, Sam, Walt Disney died during a time of greater scientific possibility. He was able to have his body frozen until medical science could advance enough to cure or manage his disease which, during your life and time frame was, shall we say, not yet available?"

Clemens quickly looks Disney up and down and, with an impish grin exclaims, "Yer frozen? Naked and frozen somewhere?"

Disney laughs and nods. He begins to shuffle aimlessly about the room, looking here and there for possible small tools easily available—just in case a need arises—finally, his tour complete, he stands ready to take the next step.

Sam is no longer reluctant, "Let's go! This is something I wouldn't miss! Only—you are in charge of overseeing this infant entity. Age brings with it some built-in pluses, and not having to deal with novices is one of the best."

Gabriel hands a sparkling round crystal to Eepia. She reverently cradles it in her hand as he explains, "Eepia, this is a portable connection to the Akashic Records. It contains accounts of every earthly event for the past 50 years, including major situations that cannot and must not be altered. It will glow and emit a particular sound when either man oversteps his limits; even you are accountable. Immediately remind them to stop and let the past continue as it should have, or else suffer possible dire consequences."

"Yes, Eepia understand cause and effect; as above so below."

Disney asks, concerned, "Will she be visible to the people we meet? Will they see and hear her?"

"Not in this present form. She is visible only to you two. With earthly experiences and under your tutelage, she will become recognizable as a fine, upstanding young lady."

Clemens walks over to the larger pond, pulls out the large jewel from his pocket and tosses it back—but immediately picks it up again and scratches a deep gash in one of the nearby walls' reflective surfaces to verify it is a true diamond. He smiles, satisfied, gives a thumbs-up sign and tosses it onto the glittering pile. It lands with a thud and sets off a cascade, a tiny avalanche of sparkles. "When I left earth, I was feeling alone and old. Useless. I resented having nobody to play with anymore. I never wanted to be a grown-up ... let alone an old grown-up. Yes, I have a hankerin' to go along with you, Walt my boy."

Grinning at Clemens' thoughtfulness, Disney responds, "Sam, I'm delighted. Besides, it might include a visit to one of your own previous haunts ... to be determined."

Walt's mind is already calculating a possible prank to pull on his long-time mentor and confidant.

"Maybe in Connecticut?" Clemens reminisces, "It was safe and quiet there, even had my own think-tank room! Oh, such sweet surrender. Lots of memories there ... and I was busy on other projects, overseeing my book sales, watching out for my daughters who were still alive, Livvy too."

"As I recall," Disney asks, already knowing the answer, "didn't you predict your own demise?"

He smiles a broad grin, "It was in 19-aught-nine, I remember it clearly still; after all, I was there to prognosticate it."

He points to himself, inflating his ego, "With absolute authority I quote myself: I came in with Halley's Comet in 1835. It is coming again next year, and I expect to go out with it. It will be my life's greatest disappointment iffen I don't go out with it. I was right, declared dead the day after the comet reached its closest approach to earth, ending the supposition about my death being greatly exaggerated by all news sources."

He turns to Gabriel, "Okay, Gabriel, how do we do this?"

"It is all taken care of, I think. Wait a moment, let me check." He touches the large crystal obelisk on his desk gently; the room shifts from pink to blue.

That deep, resonant voice permeates everywhere, "Yes, Gabriel?"

"Are there any last-minute instructions for our three travelers?"

"Yes-s-s. Enjoy yourselves and learn all that you can. And Samuel, try to behave—cancel that. Be yourself. Remember Walt's in charge, it'll be less stressful for you. And Walt, before you go, try your best to suspend any disbelief, OK? Enjoy the journey."

Disney nods in acknowledgement.

A sparkling radiance encompasses them. Twinkling lights shimmer from above, surrounding the three shapes; they dissolve into timelessness.

Gabriel looks concerned, almost sad, as he watches them dissolve into sparkling light.

Clemens reminds Disney as their forms shift, "As a journalist of some renown, I say to you ... use the five W's: who, what, when, why, where, and how. And keep it simple."

Disney thinks to himself during the relocation, Okay Walt, what's my mission during this first jump back to earth? What can I glean from this time-frame experience? Will I get the deeper message, if any shows up?

"Oh, I nearly forgot," Gabriel calls out to them, knowing full well they will hear him, "Sam, you do realize Eepia is now under your tutelage, to help you earn at least some positive merit points. Who knows, she may even help to neutralize your current deficits. Have an excellent adventure."

A loud anguished cry is heard from Sam.

Walt grins, but feels a twinge of anxiety because he realizes he must become a compassionate moderator of sorts and be an empathetic bridge between a stubborn curmudgeon and a totally innocent new soul.

∞

CHAPTER 3

San Francisco, March 1968

*I*T'S midafternoon in the Haight–Ashbury district. Fog has already settled in, the street is filled with people, especially hippies (both Hawks and Doves) and street vendors selling their wares. Samuel Clemens materializes in his usual white attire, his unlit cigar in hand, dangerously close to the curb. The shower of sparkles dissipates and he is as solid a presence as everyone else on the street.

Walt Disney appears on his right, gaping with astonishment.

They lock eyes and break into spontaneous delighted giggles.

Clemens grabs hold of a NO PARKING signpost with one hand and swings in circles around it.

Walt turns his face to the sun as it filters through the growing mist and squints, smiling in recognition. A familiar cityscape.

Clemens runs to a window of a laundromat, exhales on it and shouts with glee when moisture fogs the surface after each gust of breath.

Walt kneels and pets a black cat sleeping nearby, which responds with affection.

They are feeling bliss, almost out of control.

Eepia's indistinct, misty purple form hovers blandly, and she is still holding the crystal. Although her face is not visible, the two men sense she is studying their every movement and intention.

They choose to ignore her.

A long-haired hippie in too-tight pants, shirtless, but wearing a long-fringed deerskin vest, is lying on his side on the sidewalk, obviously under the influence of whatever dope he's been smoking. He witnessed Clemens and Disney appearing out of nowhere. He reaches over and tugs on Clemens's pant leg. "Far out, man!! How'd you do that? I mean, right on!!"

Just as Clemens starts to answer, another man with hair to his shoulders approaches and flashes the peace sign. A young girl with long stringy blonde hair hands Clemens a daisy and drapes herself limply around his shoulders. He is dumbfounded.

Disney is mortified.

Eepia's energy swirls slowly now—the atmosphere around them physically affects her too.

Clemens is the first to find his voice, "W-where are we?"

Disney looks around for clues and fishes a crumpled newspaper from a dented moss green litter can. "I can't believe this!" he says, incredulity coloring his voice. "This is San Francisco in 1968. I haven't even been dead a full two years and … what has happened to the world?"

Clemens, ignoring the wraith of a girl around his neck, cautiously asks, "Am I to understand that all of this happened because you died?"

"No. I didn't mean it that way. This was predetermined, remember? At least Gabriel led me to believe that's so."

"Good. I was searchin' for a proper response to your way of thinkin' … your ego would have taken a bit of a bruisin'."

"This has got to be an elaborate joke on me, Sam. I know I was known for playing games with other people's minds. But I've been gone barely two years."

"Gabriel is a fun guy, but never known for his practical jokes, you know what I mean? I think we're dealing with facts here."

Disney surveys the busy street, "What could have caused this … degradation?"

Sam shrugs, but the girl stays attached, so he puts his unlit cigar into his mouth and snorts, "It's like the denizens went back to caveman mode since I left the scene. This new culture … I'm not so certain humanity has been putting its time to valuable service. This is remarkable!"

Disney stands frozen in place, bewildered by the people and sounds.

Clemens extricates himself deliberately and firmly from the young girl's arms around his shoulders and props her against a parking meter.

A friendly looking black man exits a nearby grocery store. He nods to Clemens and Disney, shakes his head sadly and sniffs the air permeated by lingering marijuana smoke. "These damn hippies! Will this ever get better?"

"Who are these folks?" Clemens asks, "Don't people have mirrors nowadays?"

The man surveys the overcrowded area and raises his eyes to the sky, frustration and pain on his face. "Sure … they have mirrors. They use them for lines of cocaine … or use 'em to make sure they look as disgusting as possible. Take my kid. We used to be great pals. I took him everywhere with me. I even arranged for him to meet Willie Mays. We were tight."

Disney is genuinely excited, "You've met Willie Mays?"

"Who's Willie Mays?" Clemens inquires, obviously curious.

The shopper can't believe he hasn't heard of him; he stares in surprise at Clemens but ignores their questions. "My son announced he's no longer a Negro, or African American, but BLACK. Big surprise! He left home to join his "brothers." These hippies he considers his brothers?! Now he's living at the ocean, on the beach, in a tent! With several others of his like and kind."

Disney's empathy shines in his face as he listens.

"I was a bit of a rebel myself," Clemens says, ever ready to pontificate, "Kids take chances and make decisions they will draw on down the line. I don't regret my experiences, although I do wish it had been easier on those who loved me." He acknowledges the man's anguish and reassures him, "Not to worry, he'll be back."

"Not this kid." The shopper is disgusted. "He says he's gonna 'find' himself. Says he has lost respect for everything that his mother and I stand for. You may as well rip out our hearts...." The pain brings tears to his eyes. He looks away, pretending to adjust his shopping bags.

Eepia wants to understand, "What is man doing? He water his face?" Only Disney and Clemens hear her.

Clemens frowns and mutters, "See why I wasn't anxious to have a layman along?"

The shopper looks confused, then insulted. "Sir, I may be a layman, but I defy you to find anyone with more experience."

"I wasn't talking about that or you," Clemens removes the cigar from his teeth and quickly counters, "I was talking about a ... uh, well just trust me, I didn't make that comment in reference to you or your painful situation. You have my complete sympathy."

Disney inserts himself into the conversation, "He was trying to understand why a friend of ours made these travel arrangements. It has nothing to do with you. Our hearts go out to you."

"Whatever happened," Clemens, his wit ever intact, retorts, "it appears it has crossed color lines, not to mention intelligence zones."

A bead-bedecked man with a huge, curly Afro walks up and, smiling broadly, tousles Clemens' hair. He flashes him the thumbs-up approval sign. "Cool, man! You're a far-out dude for an old guy."

He strolls down the street with a pleased expression. The beads flash around his neck while he uses a wide-toothed hair pick on his hair, coaxing each strand to stand as far away from his scalp as possible.

A more than amply filled pair of blue bell-bottom pants steps past our travelers into their line of sight and undulates down the sidewalk.

Clemens is speechless as he watches a voluptuous young woman—the person in the tight jeans—catch up with the young man and passionately caress him. He hurriedly picks her up and moves them into an alley, out of view.

Scanning their vicinity, Clemens realizes the people around them are engaging in varying stages of lovemaking.

"What are we doing here?" Disney asks with disbelief. "This isn't what I want to see! What's the matter with these kids?"

The disgruntled shopper answers, "This is their way to protest all we have done wrong. Free love. Sex, drugs, and rock 'n' roll is their motto. No emotional ties. These are the new rules. They swallow every type of pill they can get, just to escape the reality we created."

Disney can't believe his eyes, "Don't they realize we create our own reality, like it or not, the law of cause and effect?"

"If you listen to them, we are both. Their bathing and hygiene habits are bleak at best. I imagine some think they are stone-cold allergic to a shower or tub, maybe even the Pacific Ocean, or any water. They never bathe!" The shopper pinches his nose and grimaces to make his point. "A person isn't safe on the streets anymore. It's not just religious cults dancing and demanding money, it's kids running nude across our lawns. I think the wife and I are going to move. Emily doesn't deserve it. We're good people. I just don't know where to go!"

"It seems to me," Disney wonders, "anywhere else in the world might be more wholesome. How could San Francisco let this happen? It can't be happening anywhere else, right?"

A young freckle-faced teenage girl walks up to Disney, stops in front of him and paints a psychedelic pink flower on his face with three strokes of her brush. She admires her handiwork, "There now, that's a much better look."

Startled and indignant, he immediately rubs it off with his handkerchief, not caring to see what she had done.

Eepia registers emotion, "Ahh, pretty flower." Both Disney and Clemens look in her direction, surprised, and choose not to reply.

The shopper has been watching the travelers closely and asks, "What's wrong with you guys? You been on the moon?"

Clemens grins impishly, "Yer close but not yet deserving of a cigar."

"I'm sorry. Didn't mean that disrespectfully, but how on earth could you have missed all of this? Like cockroaches, these people are everywhere, an infestation."

"I may be dense," Disney agrees, "but I still don't understand the purpose."

"Ah yes, the purpose." The shopper explains, "They say they will finally bring peace to the world. They honestly believe their perverted behavior can make that happen."

"That's what this is about?" Clemens jumps in, "Peace?"

"Peace. That's it." The shopper is caught up in his own litany, "They denounce and show no respect for us folks who fought in wars. And they have even turned their backs on the kids who are still out there dying. They refuse to be drafted. Some are going so far as to move to Canada so they won't be called up to fight for their country." His emotional energy evinces the pain this causes him.

A couple of doors away, a man in his twenties wraps an American flag into a diaper over faded jeans.

Shaking his head in disgust and despair, the proud shopper turns, nods to Clemens and Disney and then hurries away through the crowd murmuring to himself, "His voice, there's something about it. I've heard it many times, but can't put my finger on it. And the older one ... he could be the double of the guy promoting the archives at U.C. Berkeley. I wonder what they're really up to over there."

Disney sadly watches a grubby child as she digs through the gutter. Her blank-faced mother is dressed in a filthy poncho and a long, frayed skirt. She rocks back and forth against a trash barrel, barely registering, as the little girl scavenges for food.

Another young woman sees the child's plight, crouches beside her and hugs her to her side while handing her an overripe banana. The child eats ravenously.

"Where are their parents?" Disney feels more anger than frustration, "How can these people succumb to this degradation?"

Clemens decides he needs answers.

He walks over to a man sitting on the sidewalk, resting against the exterior wall of a nearby laundromat. He sports a wild beard, wears faded jeans and a shirt many times too large for him, both adorned with embroidered colorful flowers and peace symbols.

Eepia looks at him and wonders aloud, a smile in her voice, "How that shirt look on me?"

Disney and Clemens both think she would not wear it well, because she has no visible form. It would look like a shirt waving about in a gentle breeze with no apparent support.

The lounging man looks up at Clemens, pats the sidewalk beside him, and motions for him to sit down. He offers him a hit of his joint.

Clemens demurs, "Smells a mite too sweet for my liking, but thanks anyway, I kinda like the one I'm holdin'," points to his own cigar, and accepts the invitation to sit down. He folds himself slowly into a sitting position on the hard sidewalk, grunting and groaning as he does.

Eepia follows suit. The lavender mist bends toward the ground and incorporates imitated moans and groans. She positions herself close to Clemens, which he doesn't appreciate and frowns at seemingly empty space.

Disney is amused and smiles broadly.

The seated hippie begins, "I get good vibes from you, man. Name's Rain."

Always ready with a witticism, Clemens responds, "These vibes, Rain, are they good, or are they like pesky insects or disease?"

Rain laughs, "That's good, man." He inhales on the joint, holding his breath for several seconds, and exhales slowly, saying, "You're far out. I see it's in your aura."

Clemens feels totally out of his depth and chooses not to delve further.

Instead he smiles a super-sweet, uncharacteristic grin, and nods appreciatively at the hippie. "So-o-o-o, you're a proponent of peace?"

"Aren't you?" Rain's eyes flutter, the pot is making him drowsy.

"Of course! But do you think you are doing something constructive about making it happen?"

Rain is quick to retort, "Are you?"

This irks Clemens but he quickly calms down when he sees the man is not taunting him. He is truly curious. "Quite frankly, Rain—your name is Rain? I'd say it's most unusual for a name."

"I chose it because rain is made up of all of the elements and because nothing can grow without rain." His grin is genuine. He nods, pleased with his name.

Thinking quickly, Clemens comments, "Quite frankly, Rain, I wouldn't have the minutest idea where to start to bring about peace." He effectively maneuvers control of the conversation to his signature oratory about everything and everything, particularly religion and churches.

"I suppose churches try for it, but I've always felt downright manipulated by those folks. I mean, some of the people at the heads of churches in my time swore they spoke personally with God. That they alone got his messages." He pauses to see if he has Rain's continuing attention. He does, and others nearby are tuned in too.

"Armed with this power, those fellers demanded we all do exactly as they said. I maintain now that I learned a valuable lesson as a youngster. This may or may not be appropriate to this discussion—I offer it as perspective, however."

Clemens looks pleased as he gazes at the gathering audience. He thoroughly enjoys having the ears of so many, including Disney. His eyes twinkle as he continues. "As I see it, God may very well have a golden plan of peace, which he has whispered to a few chosen folks, but I personally find the validity of its working by the time it arrives in the pulpit of a church highly suspect."

Rain replies, "That's a great analogy. I enjoyed it enormously … especially from someone your age."

Clemens's butt is getting a little sore by now, so he shifts his weight back and forth. Eepia watches intently and the mist seems to mimic his movements, although she has no a clue why he's doing it. Clemens continues his soap-box rant without giving another thought to what someone, anyone "his age" would say; he is clearly focused on making his point. "In my opinion, peace is an elusive ideal on earth. I admire you for your goals, but don't understand what you are doing to prevent wars, specifically."

Rain needs no pause before answering, his eyes light up—it's so obvious to him. "It's very simple. If you don't fight, wars can't happen."

"Yes, that's true," Disney decides to insert his own thoughts into the discussion, "But every man has a personal limit," he opined, hunkering down next to them. "If someone has a plan to harm a member of your family or a friend, you will defend them, won't you? You certainly cannot remain passive if there is a threat to a loved one?"

Rain turns to Disney, "Man, you're too hyper. Being a gay man, I have had time to consider the merits of fighting for causes. Everyone has chosen his own karma."

Clemens considers Rain curiously but decides to not comment.

Rain continues, not realizing they are from somewhere else. "Karma, man. You know, your own life lessons—each time you come back to life, you have certain lessons to learn."

Intrigued, Disney readily plays along, "Your karma is what pray tell, this lifetime?

An even broader grin brightens Rain's face, "Love. I won't harm another person, regardless of the situation."

Clemens, true to form, now baits him, "Wait a minute, young whipper-snapper, I want to hear more about this karma."

"Sure. You see, there is a place in the next world—some call it Heaven, some have other names for it—which keeps a log of everything you have done."

Clemens and Disney glance toward Eepia's lavender energy. The crystal she's holding is changing hues softly. She holds it out toward Rain. "Shall Eepia give to Rain?"

Both men stand suddenly and shake their heads no. To everyone present they appear to be interacting with empty space. Rain looks a little uncomfortable. The two realize Rain cannot see their companion.

They put on overly large smiles and settle back down.

"This place," Clemens continues, intending to shift the focus, "Are you saying every action I've ever taken is recorded … there? That's a scary thought."

Rain sits up straight; until now he has either been reclining, or lounging against the building. "Precisely. I don't want to come back to clean up my act from this lifetime. I will never kill another person, and I won't put myself into a situation where there is a likelihood that it would ever become a necessity. Being gay isn't popular nor life-threatening for me."

"I wouldn't say that it isn't popular to be gay. I consider myself to be gay at times, too." Clemens doesn't know the word's meaning has altered since his day. "But I would sure as heck become the most serious fella on the street should my family be in danger. As I see it, there's a time for good-natured humor and a time to take up arms."

Both Rain and Disney exchange amused looks, and Disney reflects quietly to himself, "How quickly the language changes meanings. I wonder how many words have different interpretations now."

Rain is adamant and clear-headed as he drives his point home, "Can't you men understand, ultimately we all have control of our own destinies?"

Disney squelches a giggle with a smirk, "Lately I've been doing some reading on the subject."

"Good for you, man. We can learn something from every segment of life. How can one justify an opinion of something, or someone, if there is no personal experience to call on?"

"Are you are suggesting we have all lived a life before this one?" Disney can't believe Rain has taken the proverbial bait.

"I believe that, yes, it makes sense to me. If you blow something up … and I mean disintegrate it, the energy of what exploded never dies. This thing called a soul—the part of us that is individual and recognizable as us alone—is pure energy. So how can it die? I believe it lives on and takes another temple, or body, after each lifetime."

Clemens' eyes are dancing. He looks to Disney as he says, "Suppose you can put in a good word for me with the man upstairs? I'd prefer a strapping young body next time. This one is not as convenient as it once was."

Disney's attention drifts to the headlines in the newspaper he's been holding. Distress registers on his face and he asks, "Are we in a war situation now?"

"Vietnam," Rain answers, and he leans back on his elbows. "It's not a declared war, but we're in it."

Clemens chimes in, "America's at war again? Don't we ever learn?"

"It seems to me I've heard a few things about Vietnam." Disney is visibly confused, "I can't say I understand what the mission is …"

Rain's eyes smolder with fire, and he readily answers, "Who needs to share *that* with the public? They say: 'Men, we are at war and your country needs you.' Nobody dares question it."

"That's so very unfair!" Disney is shocked, but asserts, "There is always a good reason. Our government works hard to keep world peace. "

Rain's immediate retort is adamant and caustic, "Yeah, sure. The good old benevolent, omnipotent government taking good care of its children." He snickers nastily.

"Listen, young man," Disney decides enough is enough. "We fought for your rights to sit here dressed the way you are, saying the obnoxious things you are saying. We bought you your freedom to do this and you are really lucky to be here."

Rain stares penetratingly into Disney's eyes.

No anger.

He is simply studying Disney's words. "You're right. I do understand that. But that doesn't mean my point isn't valid."

"W-what is your point?"

Rain starts to rise, but decides instead to stay seated. He waves his arms in a wide arc that includes the people around them, "Take these kids here. Give them a gun and tell them to kill each other. Why? Because our country needs them to do it. Do you have any idea how damaging it is to a psyche to suddenly be expected to take a life because someone you don't know and who doesn't know you tells you it is your duty or you will be jailed?"

Disney hasn't spent much time studying this aspect of war. He looks stricken, pain shows on his face, and puts his hand over his heart to soothe the hurt.

Clemens, always ready to express his opinion, chimes back in, "I wrote about war once. I got to thinking how both sides of any war know in their hearts they are right and the other fella is wrong. Each side prays to their God to help them kill the other."

Rain nods, agreeing with what he is hearing from the old curmudgeon. "Yes, exactly! Correct-a-mundo."

"So, who is God going to help? Both sides are honorable in their own opinions. Both pray feverishly and reverently, petitioning for God's intervention. I'd sure as heck not want to be God in that situation. That's got to be worse than a Baptist at High Mass."

"That's interesting man, I remember reading a similar outlook, written by Mark Twain; he kinda reminds me of you somehow. I believe it was called A War Prayer."

Sam is touched, "Huh? It was published?"

"Yes, but not until well after his death because his stand on the subject was so unpopular in his day and he wouldn't allow it to be published. A righteous little story. I found it in an out-of-the-way used bookstore in east Berkeley."

Eepia is their timekeeper. "Time short before we go. You have any more questions of Rain man Mr. Clemens?"

"No, but did we get any money for the trip?" Because Sam and Walt are the only ones who hear Eepia, Rain is baffled by this non sequitur.

Clemens reaches into his pocket, delighted to discover several dollar bills. He gets up again, moaning and groaning, and excuses himself to explore a nearby Good Humor variety store, leaving Disney to talk with Rain alone.

Eepia follows Clemens closely, mimicking his grunts and groans and matching his tone.

Rain watches Clemens leave and remarks, "He's an odd one. He keeps talking to empty space, but then, I have many friends who do that too. What's he on?"

"On?"

"Oh, never mind. I love to listen to him talk. He reminds me of an elderly Samuel Clemens who wrote under his nom de plume in the last century. Surely you would know."

Disney laughs at the absurdity of the situation and glances toward the variety store door.

....

Inside, Clemens has been busy, deciding what to purchase.

He takes several selections to the front counter and, after paying the cashier, stuffs the items into his pockets. He gazes out the front plate glass window and, surprise written all over his face, he turns and frowns toward Eepia. "Never knew a woman—be she new soul or old—to be anything less than sluggish in a store."

He winks at the clerk, "Thought she'd like to never stop browsing."

The store clerk decides the old man must be senile; he was talking as if someone was nearby.

Outside, Disney is signaling them by pumping and waving his arms about; it's obviously time to leave.

Eepia doesn't understand, "What browsing mean? Is it like the nagging moves you show me when I am telling you we must hurry?"

Clemens frowns and hurries out the front door to a mildly exasperated Disney, while unwrapping a candy bar. "So, how're we all doing?"

Eepia's misty form follows close behind and shifts back and forth between them.

Clemens displays his renegade ways by scribbling on the inside of the candy wrapper in his hand while holding the candy bar in his mouth. He ceremoniously hands the wrapper to Rain, who sees the words, "My very best to you and yours, Mark Twain" written in bold letters.

. . . .

The two men and swirling lavender mist move several blocks down the busy sidewalk, stepping around so much loose trash that it is piled up along the gutters. They board a cable car—the sign emblazoned on the side reads. "A SAN FRANCISCO TREAT."

Eepia is unnoticed, her light lavender mist hovering about like a small cloud attached to an outside seat; an errant balloon bulging a pair of what seem to be ears accompanies her. They ride for three stops and, as the car approaches the fourth, a sight piques Disney's interest, a building emblazoned with a sign: MITCHELL'S ICE CREAM PARLOR SINCE 1953.

They get off at the stop and Disney makes a beeline for it; his taste buds are clamoring for something icy cold. As they enter the parlor he scans the patrons and thinks, Now there's a nice, friendly, innocent-looking couple. He decides to treat them to an ice cream cone. He hadn't noticed two men in black suits enter the shop behind he and Clemens.

. . . .

Sherry Plaster, now a medical student, is on vacation and happily touring the San Francisco sights with her childhood friend, Suzy Fitz. Their cable car stops near an ice cream parlor and they decide to get off. Sherry steps down to the street and passes by Clemens and Disney on the sidewalk. Neither of the girls notices Eepia.

Sherry thinks one of the men looks familiar, but shakes her head and mutters to herself, "That's not possible!"

A man in a full military dress captain's uniform, his nameplate indicating his surname, Robb, holds the door for his wife as they exit the shop. He permits Suzy and Sherry to enter. The girls are gracious and say, "Thank you, that's very kind of you. We're so enjoying San Francisco, and we hope you are too! And by the way," they volunteer, "you must ride on a cable car, if you don't do anything else!"

Captain Robb's wife asks, "Honey, can we?" They see another car approaching and he smiles and nods, so they stand at the appointed stop. The two beefy men wearing black suits and sunglasses—obviously body guards—stand alert and vigilant near the couple. They frown as Sherry passes near them. Unimpressed, she utters, "And good day to you too."

Disney and Clemens have finished their ice cream cones outside Mitchell's while waiting to board the next cable car. It pulls up, they get on, and the conductor indicates empty seats. He clangs the bell vigorously.

Mrs. Robb still hasn't finished and steps on, her full attention on her ice cream cone. Her husband and the two bodyguards follow, and the car gets underway.

The large, portly cable car conductor rings the bell in a rhythmic cadence, announces the next stop, and calls "All aboard" as they pull away. He smiles at the new passengers.

Two blocks later, the conductor notices the newest female passenger is still eating her ice cream and sternly reminds her, "Ma'am, eating ice cream aboard this cable car is a violation of company policy, you must disembark immediately."

The couple and the two men in black get off at the next stop.

∞

CHAPTER 4

More from Haight–Ashbury

OUR three travelers ride a bit farther on the cable car before Sam asks, "Say, would you mind if we stop off at a library in Berkeley? I understand it has a collection of my works, or so I've been told. Could be interesting. If you have a mind to, that is."

Walt thinks about it and asks Eepia, "What does the crystal indicate, Eepia?"

She holds up the crystal and recites: "The Bancroft Library, at the center of the University of California, Berkeley, campus and its primary special-collections section houses letters, journals, and nearly 600 manuscripts of unpublished works and papers known as the Mark Twain Project."

Clemens nods his head approvingly, "Ah, yes, I do seem to recall hearing some rumblings and ruminations about it. Aptly named, if I do say myself. The collection began in 1967 with the intention of including everything written by me, supposedly. I have a sense, however, that it could contain a bundle of unpublished material from my days as a newspaper writer in Missouri, and Nevada, where a relative lived, and maybe a few places in between, like San Francisco."

He turns to Disney and asks, "Walt, what do you think? No pressure of course, this is your adventure, I'm just along for the ride."

Eepia interjects, "Let Eepia finish please. Crystal also says Berkeley was the birthplace of the antiwar movement formed by the first Vietnam Day Committee in May 1965 and held a 36-hour teach-in event on campus that attracted more than 30,000 people. Soon afterward, several hundred students marched down to the Berkeley Draft Board carrying a black coffin. Students burned their draft card, an act not yet declared illegal by the U.S. Congress. This Committee also organized demonstrations along the Santa Fe railroad tracks running through West Berkeley and Oakland in sight of trains taking new inductees to the Oakland Army Induction Center. They were joined by more than 15,000 demonstrators and marched toward Oakland, where they were met by policemen in full riot gear."

Hearing this, Walt asks Sam, "Are you sure you want to go there now? What about another time when it might, let's hope, be a bit calmer, less antagonistic toward humanity?"

"Why, do you think I might stir up a smidgen of unruliness?"

Eepia insists, "Eepia not yet complete with crystal information." She raises the glowing orb again and intones, "Administrators quickly banned the Vietnam Day Committee members from on the college campus, so students took up the cause. They held sit-ins around Navy recruiters and other pro-war organizations that had set up tables in the student union."

Clemens yawns, "Looks like we're getting a history lesson, much more'n I ever thought I might need. What about we make our way to an exit of sorts?"

He winks.

Disney gets the hint, and gently reasserts himself. "Hold up, Sam, this is my trip, remember? I believe what Eepia is saying is important because it gives me fodder to think about before making my decision, OK?"

"Balderdash, boring, boring, must everything be about you?"

Angel Gabriel's voice rings out suddenly and counsels Clemens, "Now hear this: Sam, this is Walt's trip, as you must recall, you're here only because the Man Upstairs has agreed to it at my request. Don't blow it! I expect you to honor your commitment."

"Harrumph! Oh, all right."

"Good. Let Eepia finish the record."

Clemens comments snippily, his effort at gallantry completely hollow, "Yes, Eepia, please continue, if you must."

Her swirling mist is subtly changing, "Yes, thank you. Mr. Clemens, crystal not done. A campus protest of the Dow Chemical Corporation took place on Berkeley's campus in 1966. They produced something called napalm. In 1967, organizers of Stop the Draft Week, along with 3,000 demonstrators, focused on the Oakland Army Induction Center. More than 10,000 demonstrators attended, and protestors handed out leaflets to the inductees, asking them to change their minds and refuse to serve.

"By 1968, the antiwar movement's goal of making the war visible to mainstream America had succeeded. Public opinion polls from 1965 showed that most Americans supported the war; they were known as Hawks. In three short years, those numbers were reversed and the opposition became known as Doves, or Peaceniks.

"The North Vietnamese, despite being seen as ready to give up the war, were able to launch a massive attack in January 1968 called the Tet Offensive. It was a major move on the enemy's part that resulted in far too many casualties, mainly Americans.

"President Johnson's reelection was challenged by two antiwar candidates, Senators Bobby Kennedy and Eugene McCarthy, and ultimately he chose not to run for re-election. Vice President Richard Milhous Nixon was elected president in 1968 and continued the war through his aborted second term."

Disney has been intently listening, taking it all in, and suddenly catches his breath, "An aborted second term? I wonder what that was, err, is all about? Sam, since you are a wise, educated author of some fame, do you know anything about aborted presidents?"

Clemens deliberately has not been paying much heed, but manages to address the question, "Not so's you'd notice, I imagine. I'd have to recollect some and that can be a test for my memory. If need be, I could check my writings in that library over across that body of water."

Disney glances over the Bay, "Well, after giving it due consideration, the answer is no. I think it better we pass on your respectful request. Petition denied."

Strange tingling sensations began, felt by our travelers, the first indication they would soon transfer to another time and place. Fortunately, the cable car came to its next stop just in time for the three to disembark. Disney addresses the conductor, "Thank you, this ride has been unlike anything at Disneyland and I love the most unusual cadences of your bell ringing and announcing."

A seasoned veteran of the cable car company, the conductor says, grinning, "Got the best-of-the-best award three years running now. Learned reggae growing up in Trenchtown, Jamaica, and played with the rhythms 'till I got what I like." He laughs heartily, smiled at Disney and Clemens, resumed clanging his bell, and sauntered down the length of the car, merrily talking up a storm to the remaining passengers.

A vortex of energy swirls around them and they disappear in broad daylight. Two drugged-out hippies are enthralled at the sight. Not certain their altered state is to blame, they manage to comment in unison, "Far out, man!! How'd they do that? I mean, right on!!"

One looks at the other, "Jinx, you owe me another sugar cube!" They both begin giggling, which quickly escalates into a laughing fit that takes them to their knees, holding each other up.

Clemens reaches for a pen in his coat pocket, scribbles on the inside of another crinkled candy wrapper, which floats out of the shimmering vortex to the sidewalk, bearing the words, "My very best to you and yours, Mark Twain.".

As the last of their physical mass disappears, he says delightedly, "That oughta confuse them."

....

While in the void, Disney evaluates his first excursion back on earth. He hears Gabriel's voice in his mind, "OK, Walt, what did you learn so far?"

After some silent reflection he thinks aloud, "Well, right from the start things are definitely not what they were. Love is in the air, but also fear and war. I'm not judging the attitude of free love, whether it's good or not; that's up to society to decide how long it will last. I've seen polarized ideologies, that is, Hawks versus Doves, and what seems to be a free-love society that advocates noncommitment. Bohemians renamed themselves hippies and the culture is in full swing, at least where we were in the Bay Area of California. This may be the harbinger of things to come, right?"

Silence.

He continues, "This may be harder than I previously thought. It's one thing to view conditions from a distance and see life on earth through the viewer in Heaven; but it's another being immersed in the thick of it. One's clothing choices or not to wear clothes at all is up for debate. And finally, I've heard something about an aborted second term of office for the President."

Gabriel replies telepathically, We shall see, won't we? He addresses all three aloud, startling them, "Now, Sam, I'm glad I decided to add a monitoring system during your excursion. Don't you remember the warnings about potentially interfering with the timeline?"

Clemens answers sheepishly, "Err, yes, I seem to recall something like that … and?"

"We cannot overlook that during this first excursion you have managed to interfere and create a potential hiccup in the time continuum. By leaving written evidence behind, what you said might have ramifications down the road that you alone will have caused, and that may or may not be a good thing. Do not do it again, understand?"

"Yes, of course Gabe."

"Eepia, from now on, you are to be more aware of Sam's intentions. This is why you are in charge of the crystal. Did you not notice it changing color when he first wrote the note to Rain?"

"Eepia sorry, do better."

"Good, good. OK then, Walt, where next?"

Still trying to make sense of this first adventure, Disney answers politely, "I think in some instances being here is so different from before that to me it feels as if I'm a sojourner on a foreign planet for reasons yet unknown, or something like that."

Gabriel laughs, "Change is inevitable, and growth is optional. It's all in how you choose to experience it."

∞

CHAPTER 5

Not of this Earth

GRAY sand and rocks litter the barren landscape. Piles of boulders are scattered about helter-skelter, none in any particular order. An outstretched American flag marks the astronauts' visit, and the bottom section of the Eagle—Apollo 11's Lunar Module—stands empty, incapable of re-entering Earth's atmosphere, but the ascent stage rockets toppled the flag as the Eagle lifted off.

Visible in the black sky, following an explosive burst, the trail of the Eagle's ascent stage extends far above into the emptiness. It will return to Earth once it has connected with Apollo 11.

A lone lunar surface television camera is trained on the scene, operated remotely by the technicians in NASA's Spacecraft Center Mission Control.

Suddenly, tumbling and half-floating images of two men and one person-sized bundle of energy unexpectedly appear. Clemens, Disney, and Eepia come to a standstill and their eyes follow the path of the departed spacecraft upward. They are thoroughly confused.

As they look around, they are awestruck by the extraordinary view of the large blue planet in an otherwise black sky.

All their movements must take the moon's reduced gravity into account. They slowly look around the lifeless moonscape.

Disney is mildly agitated, "I can't believe this, you made us late for our transfer assignment, Sam. We should have been here five minutes earlier."

"So, this is our punishment? Gabriel sends us to, to ... what I assume is the place where all good politicians go when they die?"

Disney looks to Eepia, hoping for answers. "Does that thing you're holding still work? Can it tell us where we are?"

Eepia's form has coalesced into something distinctively hippie-like. A face is almost visible. We can clearly discern the outline of long hair, a poncho, and boots. "Yes, I will translate." she holds the crystal up to her forehead. "Moon landing. July 20th, 1969."

Disney is thunderstruck, "Moon landing? This is absolutely wonderful!"

"What? We are on the moon?" Clemens declares, "This the perfect place for all deceased politicians. Great place for them to ponder all of the bedlam created at their hands."

Disney looks upwards pointing, "Look. That must be the space ship! Sam, had we arrived a few moments earlier, we could have seen it happen. You made us late by asking to visit your library selections across the Bay, and needing to have the last word. Next time keep it to yourself, OK?"

"Please ..." their hippie-looking guide protests, "let Eepia continue?"

"Of course," Disney apologizes. "I'm sorry and so is Sam!" He glares at Clemens.

"Television camera follows the Eagle's blast-off from the moon. It seems to move in slow motion back into the darkness of space. It will rejoin the command module Columbia of the Apollo 11 space flight."

Clemens and Disney raise their eyes to watch the tiny craft moving farther into space. It is almost a spiritual experience for both men; they stand silent and reverent.

Eepia continues, "Awe-filled announcers describe the event to the world. For the first time in Earth's history, a human being has actually set foot on the soil of another universe-traveling satellite. The camera the mission left behind is still operational."

Disney turns and spots the camera, mounted on the lunar rover. He is dumbfounded and overwhelmed and it shows all over his face. Sam is standing perfectly still, listening to Eepia.

"NASA instructs the camera to survey the lunar surface. The camera pauses to focus on the fixed-position United States of America flag. Tears flow from a nation so proud it is immobilized momentarily, as the flag takes on a special aura."

Disney's voice is husky with emotion, "Yes, I can certainly imagine!"

"Children announce to parents everywhere that they are going to be astronauts when they grow up. Ex-Marines and Air Force veterans wonder if they could have been Neil Armstrong, Edwin "Buzz" Aldrin, or even Michael Collins, had they channeled their energy toward that specific goal. Each is secretly convinced they could. Mothers across the world hold their collective breath for the safe return of these brave men."

She moves the crystal away from her forehead. Its report finished, the inner glow dims.

"They did it, Sam!! They actually sent men to the moon."

Sam, entrenched in his usual curmudgeonly thinking, says, "Somehow, I find it more extraordinary that they found a way to get back off of it. It seems to me I'd be more excited about leaving this desolate place."

Disney begins running to his right in slow motion. "Look!! There are footprints!! An American has actually walked on the moon! I can't begin to tell you what a thrill this is!"

Clemens considers where they are and decides it's best to be short and to the point, "There's no consarned air here!"

Disney stops and stares as Clemens sinks to his knees, obviously uncomfortable. Disney kneels beside him and pats his shoulder. "Get low to the ground! The moon's atmosphere has no oxygen in it, but the rocks should give off some."

"You want me to get down and sniff the rocks? I can't believe you just said that."

"I don't know what else to tell you to do." Disney is dismayed, "Why would they send us to a place that has no air to breathe? Where did my thought of where I wanted us to go enter into this?"

Clemens is now thoroughly enjoying himself and quips, "Whatcha worried about? Maybe I'll die? Snap out of it, Walt!"

Disney misses the point, because his emotions are still running high, "I guess I never expected it to be such a harsh and cold environment. You really are okay, right?"

"For a man who has been deceased 59-plus years, I seem to be thriving. Relax, Walt. Wait. Here, have a chocolate bar." Opening his coat, he reveals chocolate bars stuffed into every discernible place. He unwraps one quickly and offers it to Disney. "Thought I'd give up smokin' for the rest of the day."

"Eepia would like one."

Sam quickly counters, "Naw. You have to pay more attention to your girlish figure, now that you are starting to have one."

She looks down sadly, "Okay."

"Oh the infirmities of manhood! I can't deal with that tone. Have two!"

Eepia stuffs them into her mouth, paper and all. Clemens rolls his eyes, grabs them from her, peels off the wrappers and hands them back, sighing in consternation. Eepia holds the candy in both hands and slowly looks around the barren moonscape.

Sam is ready to pronounce judgment on their situation. He settles down to the ground, physically delighted at how easy it is. "It's difficult for me to believe they really have put a man on the moon. It's not so much the actual getting here that amazes me. People are a clever bunch and it seems inevitable they'd go snooping around the neighboring stars and moons. No, what astounds me is how they got around the restrictions and legalities."

"What do you mean?" asks Disney, not sure where this is going.

"I've often pondered the fate of Noah, had he lived today. I mean, there was a man without a lick of experience in boat building. He and his seven cohorts were between 100 and 600 years old. Their boat had no rudder, no anchors, no water facilities, only two windows under the eaves, no paddles, no nurses, and not even one mortician—which seems mandatory to me given the ages of the crew and, added to that, in excess of 8,000 uncaged animals."

Disney laughs and nods his understanding "I know. I studied the moon while I was earthbound. I had envisioned and actually made a device to help people experience what space travel would be like someday and installed it in Tomorrowland. Now, I'm really here. It's breathtaking!!"

Clemens, feigns a cough, "Literally."

Eepia holds the crystal to her forehead once more, "One moment please, message coming through. The three in the Eagle are rejoining the mother ship, Columbia. All are well." She continues to hold it to her forehead in case anything else comes in. Disney is amazed that where they are is like being there in real time.

....

A NASA spokesman in Mission Control keys his mic and warns, "Columbia!! We have a problem: we've sighted two bogies.... Correction, three bogies on the surface of the moon. Can you identify?"

Columbia's commander is mystified and demands, "Three bogies?"

"Affirmative. Can you help to identify?"

"No sir, we haven't the foggiest idea what you're talking about. Can you be more definite?"

The NASA spokesperson is clearly uncomfortable, "N-no. We'll get back to you."

The monitors in NASA Mission Control track the lunar camera's view of the two men. Clemens gets to his feet with ease and hurls a stone. It moves in a slow arc and sails much farther than he expects.

....

Disney's interest is piqued when he sees the camera's movement; it's tracking Clemens's actions.

Clemens stands up fluidly, unlike his actions curbside in San Francisco. He easily closes the distance to the camera in three steps and stares deeply into the lens.

The men at NASA gape in amazement as they witness a male without a space suit approach the camera and study the lens carefully.

A fuzzy picture of a moustache and bushy eyebrows looms prominently on the NASA monitors. An eye blinks, shocking the NASA personnel. They know the image is a live feed and the impossible is happening.

....

Eepia grows alarmed because the once dormant crystal now flashes brightly and she reports, "We have problem. Men at NASA already reeling from the impact of astronauts on the moon now stare at conditions that cannot possibly exist, namely two men who seem completely comfortable without breathing apparatus on an airless earth satellite. There is no possible explanation for this aberration. Nobody speaks in Mission Control. Heads swivel—they reassure themselves they are not the only spectators of the unbelievable scene that continues to unfold before them."

She warns both men, "We not belong here and more important we should not be in the view of these people. We are confusing timeline."

Disney is unconcerned and curious, "What an interesting situation. I wonder what or who they think we are?"

"Who would that be?" Clemens comments as he continues to stare into the camera that monitors their every move. "Do you think maybe they are seeing us live right now? What a conundrum, eh?"

"The folks who are operating this camera," Disney chuckles, "I wonder how they rationalize we are physically on the moon."

Clemens' eyes twinkle in delight, "Don't suppose they'd take us for spooks?"

"Look! Whenever we move, the camera follows us." Disney smiles, "It is being directed to watch us by a living, breathing person! I can't tell you how exciting this is for me!!"

"Walt, think of how exciting it is for that poor fella who has to explain in detail that two ghosts are traipsing around on the moon." Clemens slaps his thigh in obvious delight. "No siree! Hope he has thought to take out some mental insurance policies. I have a feeling, call me clairvoyant if you will, but I think he is going to be ordered to get plenty of rest."

"What is spooks?" Eepia is confused and befuddled by these new concepts. "What is ghosts? Eepia not understand."

Clemens motions to her to follow him.

He moves away from Disney, now the camera monitor, rights the U.S. flag the Eagle's departure had toppled, and salutes, honoring it. He lowers himself into an Indian position, cross-legged and flat-bottomed on the dry, dusty lunar surface. "Eepia, ghosts and spooks are perhaps the scariest of all things in the universe. I personally have been witness to one of them and it is something I will never be able to heal from. I wrote about it in one of my memoirs."

Eepia is confused and huddles close to Clemens, searching his face for guidance that simply is not there. Clemens enjoys every second of her attention. "I was on a speaking tour at the time. Stayed in an old hotel in the East."

Thoroughly savoring the moment, he contemplatively bites into a candy bar and looks off toward the Earth from the moonscape, certain the effect of each pause is increasingly disconcerting to NASA. "The room wasn't comfortable. I was lying on my back, cussing the flies and mosquitoes. They had night vision, but I was pretty near sightless."

Although concerned about Eepia's revelation through the crystal, Disney finds himself being drawn into the story—he could never resist Samuel Clemens's imagination, expressed as his alter ego Mark Twain. As if magnetized, despite the excitement of being on the Moon, he draws near and kneels near Clemens, eager to hear one of his delightful stories.

The camera remains focused on the twosome—now almost threesome—watching their every action.

"The bed was lumpy, the weather very humid." Clemens carries on. "I got up to go for a walk and welcomed a light appearing from the right of my visual field. It glowed blue and I didn't find it unusual at the time, on account of its allowing me to find my shoes."

He pauses deliberately to raise the tension. While seeming to stare blankly into the darkness of space, Clemens slyly shoots a sidelong look at Eepia to check her rapt attention. "The light proceeded to gain in brightness. It was about then I honed in on it. And I was brought up short by the most horrifying of sights …"

Eepia takes a weak but audible deep breath, "Eepia confused." She wraps her nearly visible arms around bended knees, hugging herself for comfort.

"It was the mostly transparent form of a mighty buxom lady in her fiftieth year, I'd say."

Disney is now thoroughly captivated. He hunkers down beside Eepia, enchanted, and asks, "So what happened?"

"She was just standin' there, and I got the unmistakable impression she wasn't enjoying my company. I could see through her arms, her midriff … but her face …"

Eepia shudders and leans toward Disney for support; he circles his arm around her not-too-solid form. Enthralled and entertained, they momentarily forget where they actually are.

NASA's camera records their movements and Mission Control personnel are mesmerized by their actions, although unable to comprehend what they're seeing.

"Her face was as solid as China and mean-lookin' as anything I've ever encountered. I started to stand. Not to run, mind you, but out of sheer respect for womanhood—in politeness."

Disney laughs heartily at this, rocking back and forth on his haunches. Clemens remains poker-faced, although it is obvious he is enjoying the effects of his biggest talent: storytelling. "Anyway, she motioned me to stay seated. I affirmed that was all right by me. My legs wouldn't have supported me at that moment, anyhow. I inquired, 'Are you a ghost?' She said, 'Now what do you think, Sonny?' There was such sass in her tone, I bristled and found myself downright shouting, 'I think you are persnickety, 'n I think yer a ghost!'"

Eepia moves closer to Disney for comfort.

Delighted with her reaction, Clemens leans toward her and, in a low, sinister voice, purposely calculated to unnerve her, "She leaned her face into mine and said, seething, 'You ain't seen nothing yet!'"

Disney remains spellbound. Neither he nor Eepia can take their eyes off him.

Clemens shudders dramatically while inhaling deeply, as if it takes all his strength to go on.

"I drew myself up to full size and tried real hard to puff out a he-man chest, so as to intimidate this woman-ghost. She wouldn't have any of it and remained aloof. Even appeared to be amused. I was becoming impatient. My walk was waiting and she was showing no signs of leaving. I demanded an explanation, 'If yer a ghost, why then are you here bothering such a … God-fearin' gentleman, I ask you that?'"

He pauses again to survey his tale's impact; he can't hide his enjoyment of their horrified reaction. He looks away to regain his composure and nods toward the camera, "She seemed to be gaining in orneriness with each passing second. 'Men! You always need an explanation for why we ladies do things. I can simply be here because I chose to come. I need no other reason … but I do have one. I want to be assured you will remember me.' I told her I didn't see how that would be a problem."

Disney is smiling again. He enjoys Clemens's self-effacing humor. The humbler and more human, the more endearing he is.

"She continues to leer at me and talk … and I continue to pay homage to her words, the best I can muster. 'You will have an occasion in the future to remember me.' Once again, I told her I doubted I'd quickly be forgetting her. She said it was imperative that I didn't, for the sake of someone near to her who needed the reassurance of survival after the flesh."

"Interesting phrase, after the flesh." Disney considers the connotation.

Eepia doesn't know what to say, she remains mute, studying both men for clues how to respond. Clearly anxious, she wraps her arms around herself even tighter for protection—but from what? She has yet to figure that one out.

"Disgustin' is what it was." Clemens muses, "None of that sounded appetizing to me and I was just hoping she'd go back to wherever she'd come from. After all, if she could survive the flesh's demise ... who's to say I wouldn't be called upon by a particularly angry cow who hadn't resolved the idea that I enjoyed a rather large steak before retirin'?"

Disney winces at the thought.

Eepia stares penetratingly into Clemens' face, hers absolutely blank.

The NASA camera is focused on Clemens' animating gestures and form and catches his every movement.

"She kept on whining about us men and how we keep women shackled to demeaning jobs and such. I finally told her to lobby somewhere else for someone who cared. That wasn't at all pleasant of me, I know, but neither was it very relaxing to know that at any moment a person could open the door to that hotel room and see me nose-to-missing-nose with a ghost. At that, she disappeared."

"She just disappeared?" Disney is involved hook, line, and sinker.

"Like cigar smoke. I have never shared this with anyone. On account of my reputation of tottering on the shredded edge of reality." He looks candidly about for reactions from his audience.

"Eepia no like cigar smoke."

Disney is amused at her unfailing naïveté then disregards it to ask, "Did you ever hear from her again?"

Clemens nods, "Unfortunately, yes. It was at a séance at my dear friend and neighbor's, Harriet Beecher Stowe. I was always intrigued with the idea of spirits and such. Her sister was having some folks over for a séance, so I wangled myself an invitation."

"What is séance? Eepia has much to know. I want to learn and understand all I can as quickly as possible."

Clemens is close to losing patience with her interfering and naïveté and, irked, he doesn't bother to explain. "Moments after we were all seated, what they called a "presence" entered the room. We all honestly felt her near. Then a voice shouted from the mouth of the medium, 'Sammy, I told you we'd be seein' each other again. You do remember me at the hotel?' I nodded vigorously; the memory was all too vivid. 'I want you to describe me to the gentleman on your right, and do a good job of it, or I'll be refreshin' your memory!'"

"It was the same?" Disney couldn't help himself, "The ghost from the hotel?"

Clemens beams, then nods and shifts his weight to get more comfortable. "Well ... adjectives fairly flew from my lips! There was no way I ever wanted to be seein' that woman again. The man was pathetic. He sat right beside me and cried all over himself."

He pauses dramatically. "Humiliating, that's what it was. He sobbed that it helped him immensely to know his wife was still alive in spirit. I told him it would have helped me personally to know that woman had disappeared altogether! Don't think he heard me, though."

"At least you had a witness to your encounter … at the séance." Disney decides to relate one of his own experiences. "My ghostly episode occurred when I was all alone."

Clemens is excited, "You!? You've seen a ghost, Walt? A real one?"

"Other than the one I'm addressing right now?" Disney chortles.

"I don't count. I am not really a certified spook. I'm just along for the ride, remember? I want to hear something that will scare the soup out of me. Come on man, tell me!"

She cringes, "Eepia not want soup scared out of her."

"I won't embellish this for your sake, Eepia, unlike our former raconteur, but I can unequivocally say it was interesting. I was in my early teens, out on a walk one morning. Through the trees I saw a large man positioning himself directly in the path in front of me."

Clemens can't help himself, "Was he headless?"

Disney is startled by the question. "N-no."

"Was he or it carrying a dagger? … chains? … moaning?"

"No, no! He looked just like any other man—taller maybe. He wore a long coat, not unlike what I envision Abe Lincoln wearing in his prime."

"Humph. Any ghost worth his salt carries at least a chain or two." Clemens is unimpressed.

"Really? Where's yours?"

"I don't count, I said … and I didn't have time to prepare. No sir, I'm very disappointed in your ghost."

"Well, this changed my whole life," Disney is adamant, "so in my opinion it was a quality encounter. Odd though, now that I look back on it, I realize it was an overwhelmingly powerful experience. I'm amazed I stashed it in my subconscious for all of those years and never shared it. I guess sitting here on the moon is as good a time as any."

Clemens becomes impatient, he wants to know, now. "Share it!! I'm not getting any younger, y'know, and I don't want to be transported off this lunar landscape before I hear."

"Eepia not getting younger, too."

"Oh, all right," Disney continues, "The man in front of me was close to 6 feet 3 inches tall, I'd estimate. He shook his head at me, a stern expression on his face."

Clemens always must contribute a few choice comments regardless of the situation, or who he is in the conversation with, or where they are. "Good!! A hideously stern expression on his face. That's good. Go on."

"It wasn't a hideously stern expression, Sam, it was more like the look a person sees on his father's face when he is being ordered not to disobey."

"Walt, this is getting to be bo-o-oring." Clemens rolls his eyes skyward.

Disney looks at him squarely, "Well-l-l ... it wasn't boring to me. I swear, all of the hair stood up on my arms and at the back of my neck. The man would not let me pass. His will was as strong and as impossible to resist as if it were a solid brick wall in front of me. I reluctantly turned to walk in the opposite direction, then glanced back over my shoulder ... just as he faded away. I ran home so fast, my body had a hard time keeping up with my feet."

"I've experienced that kind of fear a time or two." Sam is interested now. He waits to see if it elicits any reaction, but seeing none he motions with his arms for Disney to continue.

"The next day, I learned that a young boy had been murdered by a deranged lady at the same time—mere minutes' difference at the most—and place that the ghost had appeared to me. Well, I believe he saved my life."

"Did you ever find out who he was?"

"Several years later, I was working on a cartoon for a company. I was in the local library, and I was stunned to find a photograph of the man who saved me."

Walt waits to see if Sam is really intrigued. He is. "Who was he?" It seems an eternity before Walt continues.

"He had been a minister. He was killed by a runaway horse in the same area that I encountered him. He'd died several years before he appeared to me. It touched me deeply when I discovered this. I made a silent vow I would do something special with the life he had returned to me."

"Never knew until now that ghosts got to have gooseflesh. Here, look at these!" Clemens pulls up his sleeve and shoves his arm under Disney's nose. Eepia does the same, showing him her solid arm adorned by a bracelet of beads from their San Francisco experience.

Disney scoots backward, good naturedly shaking his head, not really wanting to look. He winks at Eepia and then turns his attention back to Clemens, who is sitting expectantly, chomping on another Hershey bar. "Maybe another time perhaps. How'd we get on this subject anyway?"

"We were imagining what the folks behind that viewing contraption must be seeing" he waves his arms to indicate their surroundings, "Three ghosts on the moon."

"Three ghosts on the ... yes-s-s! That's right! We are actually on the moon. The people of the entire earth must be savoring this moment; I hope as a uniform body. I must think that peace will come only when humans realize they are one species in the universe. One among millions of others and they must link together to survive as a unit."

Clemens blows a kiss impishly toward the camera. "Lend me your pen. The writing one."

Disney finds one in a pocket and hands it over, hesitantly, "And for what if I may ask this time?"

He grabs it from Disney's hands, "This oughta confuse 'em ..." He gets up and glides to the American flag. Holding it in one hand, he writes: "My very best to you and yours, Mark Twain.'

Disney is getting decidedly irritated at his companion, he doesn't want to abruptly end any of his 50 years of experiences. "I wish you would stop doing that! Look at the crystal, it's is very red and beeping again."

Clemens grins impishly, "Persnickety little contraption, isn't it?"

Walt angrily takes the pen back, shoves it into an inside pocket. "Our agreement is not to leave any evidence we have been traveling in time. So far, you have done it twice before, and we have been cautioned by Gabriel—you know, the angel who is making this trip possible? No more please! You are hindering my decision-making process. Do you insist you are who you are and not aware of the significance of these opportunities?"

"OK. I'll be good," Sam acknowledges rather condescendingly under his breath, "Here, share a candy bar with me. Consider it a peace offering."

Walt hesitates before accepting the peace offering, "Oh, all right. Sam, it's just that we have so much time to search through, and I don't want you to blow it for yourself, and especially for me. "

"Here's..." as he breaks the bar, "... uh ... not quite half ... call it interest. Enjoy."

Savoring the chocolate, the two men are drawn to gaze at the spectacular beauty of the Earth from space. Everywhere they look the heavens are black and amazing stars twinkle their radiance.

Eepia holds the flashing crystal to her head, once again explaining its pulses. "The camera zooms in on the men and another obscured figure. A small group of technicians in NASA's Mission Control Center stare numbly at the screen. Each is unable to speak. In silent, mutual agreement, each slinks to his own respective desk, never to speak of the hour's vigil again. Personal credibility depends on this silence."

The two men on the moon feel the sparkles surrounding them and realize they are about to leave. Clemens reflects back to being severely admonished, returns to the upright flag and lowers it gracefully, reverently, back onto the cold moon's surface, "Sorry 'bout that; gotta keep things from goin' too far off kilter. Them's the rules, ya know." They move closer to Eepia to transfer as a unit. They watch the blackness of space in amazement, as the transfer initiates. She looks at the crystal; which indicates time is still available before the hour is up. "Mister Disney, there's still some time left in this period; is there anything you would like to visit or see?"

Without a moment's hesitation, he says excitedly, "Time left? Good. As a matter of fact, I remember a musician, Joan Baez, I liked her music. Where might she be in this time period?"

Clemens impishly glances toward the camera and drops a candy wrapper from his pocket. We see the moonscape, Mark Twain's autograph on the stiff flag, and the NASA camera follows the trajectory of the wrapper as it floats slowly down onto the lunar surface.

In a shower of strobe-like lights, they are swept away in a swirl of energy.

CHAPTER 6

Woodstock

THE air is heavy with marijuana stench–sweet and skunky—and Lord knows what else.

The three materialize behind a grand stage overlooking a sea of smoke, haze, and people in all stages of dress and undress. Disney is taken aback and exclaims, "My Heavens! I cannot believe what I'm seeing. There must be hundreds of thousands of those hippies here! So many more than I could have ever imagined. And I thought San Francisco was overrun."

He turns to Eepia, "Where and why are we here?"

Eepia holds up the crystal and says, "This is a three-day celebration; we are at the Woodstock Sound Festival in the Catskill Mountains, New York. August 16, 1969. The time is 1:50 a.m. and Joan Baez is playing her last two songs for the night. You did say Joan Baez, yes?"

He nods, "Thank you Eepia, yes, I did wish to see or hear a certain folk singer I had heard in the 60s, before coming aboard as Heaven's Creative Director."

Clemens is astounded, "Iffen I'm correct Walt, you asked—and so shall you receive, as the good book says." He sneaks a peek from backstage at the throng of amassed people. "There seems to be quite the cacophony assembled; in my day, there weren't ever that many in one place at any one time, compared to all those out there now, 'cept maybe at a cold, dreary inauguration or two."

"Crystal indicates over 400,000 in attendance," Eepia announces, "Anything else you want to know?"

Neither one says anything; they are simply in awe of the spectacle before them.

Eepia slides the crystal into the side pocket of a discarded dashiki left lying askew; now adorning her person, it fits just right.

For the first time, she has a recognizably total physical form.

Ms. Baez's hair is cropped short, she wears a light paisley print shift (skimming her six-month pregnancy), a scarf wound around her neck. Guitar in hand, she's sitting on a stool addressing the audience. "For one of my last songs, it was first recorded in 1909. I'm certain you'll recognize it for its sweetness. Here goes."

The melody of "Swing Low Sweet Chariot" is instantly recognizable and directly humbles Clemens; he heard it first back then on an early Edison phonograph. "It's even better now than when I first heard it. How did she know?"

Disney is confused, "How did she know what, Sam?"

"How did she know it was a favorite of mine?"

Rolling his eyes upwards in mock anguish, "My gawd man, not everything is about you. I heard her sing it and other Americana–folk oldies many times."

"Now don't get all snippy with me Walt; I cannot help but remember how much Livvy loved hearin' it." His eyes moistening at the memory, he wipes his brow and blows his nose into a handkerchief he's snatched from inside his coat pocket."

"Mr. Disney, did you make his eyes water like Rain?"

"No dear; it's showing his emotional connection to what he is hearing and remembering. You're too young yet to have such memories and feelings."

"Oh. Thank you for setting me straight, as they say." She smiles and winks. She is definitely gaining both vocabulary and experience, to the chagrin of her tutor, Sam.

The three listen intently, becoming absorbed and singing along. Many in the audience are entranced too, by the night's events.

Joan ends with "We Shall Overcome" and the assembled multitude stands immediately. They wave their arms back and forth over their heads in unison.

Walt and Sam are utterly mystified by the crowd's reaction. "I've got to ask," Disney inquires, "where did that song come from and why is everyone standing up over it? I've never seen emotional connections like that, ever … not even when my own theme song was played."

He waits, a nervous fan, as Joan takes her bows and exits the stage toward them. The closer she gets, the more on edge Eepia becomes. She feels around in her dashiki pocket, dismayed, and says urgently, "Mr. Disney, the crystal is making funny noises. I believe you are not to interfere with the timeline; please contain yourself."

"I can't help it honey, I must talk to her for a mere moment. What could possibly go wrong?"

He waves, to bring her within speaking distance. "Ms. Baez, what you just did, how did you do that? You are something powerful … and that song, I've never heard the likes of it. Where did it come from, if I may be so bold?"

Clemens is nearby, still wiping his eyes and nodding his head, unable to speak.

Joan looks twice at him and blinks in disbelief. "Am I on some kind of acid trip? What will happen to my baby?" She stops and looks directly at Clemens, "You are the spitting image of someone I've seen pictures of."

She then turns to Disney, "And your voice, it's so familiar. If my head is on straight, I'd have to say you sound just like Walt Disney before he died. I know from the times I spent listening him and watching him on TV; how can this be real?

"And you …" she looks at the swirling costumed mist that is Eepia, "what am I seeing?"

The intoxicating marijuana stench has heightened her anxiety, coupled with the shock that what she is seeing is not a figment of her imagination. It begins to show on her face.

She looks up as she hears a strong voice, clearly and distinctly; along with the others, scolding them, "Walter Elias Disney, Samuel Langhorne Clemens, and new soul, Eepia, Now you've gone and done it. The timeline you are in is nearly fractured! You must leave immediately! Say nothing! Grab one another and hold on for your lives! On my command as Gabriel, Head Archangel, be it so!"

Their three energies swirl and shimmer, moving upward, and Joan Baez watches helplessly. She mutters, "Disney, Clemens, and Gabriel, an angel from above? Me? Oh my God in Heaven, if I were ever an atheist, I'm definitely not now!"

She feels her child move within. "Gabriel … hmmm, I think it likes the sound of that! So if it's gonna be a boy, which I think it might be, then what about Gabriel?" *

In response, she feels an immediate kick from the growing personality inside. Tears well up and overflow with the understanding of the sign she just experienced.

....

Singer and political activist, Joan Baez gave birth to a son, named Gabriel Harris, in 1969.

....

Darkness is all around, and the travelers are in some sort of void. No music, no sound, only their breathing. Gabriel's booming voice rings out, stimulating all their now-raw nerve cells. "What part of do not interfere with the timeline continuum do you not understand?"

Not a peep from anyone.

Listless, they hang their heads in shame. Disney is distraught and utterly remorseful. Clemens is stoic.

Eepia is out of her league; she holds onto the crystal with both hands while trying to stop herself from shaking.

Gabriel demands an answer. "I repeat: what part of do not interfere with the timeline continuum do you not understand?"

Disney takes a deep breath and exhales slowly, "Gabriel, I take responsibility for my misguided idealism and faux pas; what might I do to recalibrate, or make amends for this?"

Gabriel comments in a loud, clear, clipped voice, "Anyone else ready to comment?"

She shudders involuntarily, "Eepia, sorry for her part; it happened so fast I not able to control situation crystal warned about. Am I to be punished? Are you sending me back before I can learn more? Mr. Clemens not interfere with timeline this time."

Clemens' head perks up, "Now I like the sound of that; apology accepted, er, humbly that is." He lowers his head trying to conceal the smirk crossing his pursed mouth.

Gabriel's retort is interrupted by a distinct and deep rumbling.

The unmistakable, almighty voice of God fills the void. "From what I discern, yes, it is Walt who is at fault, not the other two this time. I do not keep track of particular entities, unless there is much at stake, and Walt you are the highest priority. I am keeping up with every move you make and sound you utter. Do you get my drift?"

"Oh yes sir, I most certainly do." He is trying not to pee his pants, the atmosphere is so highly charged. He crosses and uncrosses his legs, grimacing in anguish. The sudden discovery of his body needing to eliminate waste is new to him.

The commanding voice continues, "Walt, I see you are in mortal discomfort; that is nothing compared to any retribution I may or may not dish out or commence. But because you did own up to your ego-based misstep, you are now strictly on probationary status. Any other infraction will most likely exclude you from participating in any decisions about your potential next term on earth, and the world may never know what that might have been; this is cause and effect in action. Are we clear on this?"

Clemens pipes up, "Sir, yes we are and I, as Walt's mentor, do solemnly promise to be ever more watchful of his actions."

"And I Eepia be more alert about timeline alterings."

Good, it's settled then. Walt, you may resume your travels." Gabriel reassumes his authority and asks, "Where and or when do you wish to explore next?"

A wave of relief ripples across his entire body and Disney speaks, "Sir, because it is my solemn duty to decide where this assemblage goes next, I choose…"

Gabriel rumbles, under his breath, "Maybe Sam has earned his first merit?"

God's voice intones, "We'll see, won't we? Carry on."

....

The darkness dissipates. They find themselves in a dimly lit reddish space where a huge neon sign flashes: PURGATORY, NOW YOU KNOW WHAT IT'S LIKE; DON'T COME BACK, YA HEAR?

Clemens glares at the words and opines, "I've been to many forlorn places in my life; this is not one I care to return to." He turns in readiness, "Walt, my boy, let's get a move on before that sign either stays lit or says something else."

The energy swirls around the three wayward travelers. They clasp hands, and Eepia holds on tightly to both men.

....

"Wow, all I did was speak about the moon in jest and look where we went!" Walt is amazed, in awe of the immense power of where his thoughts have taken them thus far—as if he hadn't realized during his time in Heaven that all thoughts are things and actions become the commonplace there.

Gabriel is first to query Walt's thoughts about their experiences on the moon and at Woodstock. "Well Walt, what about your latest adventures?"

Clemens interjects, "Yes Walt, what about it? You literally took my breath away, and we were so far from earth too. Then you wanted to listen to some folk music; I nearly gagged on the heaviest, sweet scent ever imagined. Please be more astute about conjuring up our next visit, wherever and whenever it might be, OK?"

"You are right. I simply wondered if we had made it to the moon yet, and in a flash we were there. I didn't think about the ramifications; I was just curious. Then you, Sam, conjured up one of your glorious stories and as you well know, I cannot resist one of your mesmerizing monologues."

Clemens is thrilled by how much Walt loves to hear his stories.

Walt finalizes his thoughts, "Then the visit with Joan Baez was, in my eyes, a definite impulse. I'll be more careful with my thinking in the future." Hmmm, he thinks to himself, what about my playing something on my mentor? Yes, and I know just where.

Gabriel senses the merit Sam had earned was just dismissed, "and so soon? Yes, we shall see how this turns out."

∞

CHAPTER 7

A Soundstage Experience
Like no Other

"**OK**, Sam, where and when are we?" Disney already knows the answer.

Clemens sees what looks like a younger version of himself and asks, "Eepia, please explain this. Iffen my vision is accurate, why am I looking at a younger version of myself? It has always been my belief—which I share with my dear friend Nikola Tesla, the same body cannot occupy the same space at the same time. "

Enthralled, he watches a younger, recognizably accurate version of himself sporting Twain's trademark moustache and bristling eyebrows, interacting with others around him. "This whippersnapper seems to resemble somewhat how I may have looked, only it was so long ago I would need to consult myself in the confounded ethereal record system to be certain. Do you think it is really me, or is this some type of hoodwinkin' from Gabriel, or Walt, or …" he turns to her with a sly smile, "maybe you, Eepia?"

Eepia responds matter-of-factly, "No, Mr. Clemens, according to the crystal's calculations, we are at Warner Studios in Los Angeles, California, mid-1973. Specifically, on the set of the Bonanza television series for Episode 422: Samuel Clemens (aka Mark Twain) noses around Virginia City investigating the mysterious deaths of miners, and starts an uprising by printing accusations of claim jumping and murder in the town's newspaper."

Disney feigns being confused, "Could the crystal—as you call it—be slightly off by perhaps a century or so? This does not look like anything remotely familiar to me, unless it's something like the frontier town in Disneyland? I know where that might be."

He looks around at the two-story log cabin ranch house on a massive soundstage with its soaring ceiling. Several people wear Western costumes from the mid-1800s, surrounded by film crews and various support people standing by with props and other paraphernalia. He smiles, waiting for Sam to comment.

It takes Clemens a moment, then speaks genuine incredulity, "I'll be hornswoggled, can't be possible! Although I realize that my fertile imagination over the years before my untimely demise erroneously conjured up many a semi-fact or two." He turns to Disney, "Am I to regard this as fanciful 'imagineering,' as you have mentioned in the recent past?"

Disney is clever, always has been a practical jokester, and has expected this. He sidesteps the question. "Let's take a moment to watch what is unfolding, shall we?"

He acts as if he has already forgotten he is on probation and so recently admonished by the Chief Architect of All That Is.

....

Lorne Greene, dressed for his role as Pa Cartwright, intones, "Let us begin this day with a prayer for the family of Hoss, his other real one." Grief is palpable in waves from everyone on the set.

Disney is concerned, wondering what this is about, "The air here seems very heavy, a burden lies on this group … deep sadness is everywhere, can't you feel it?"

Eepia is diligently trying to better understand the imprecision of the English language and asks, "How can air be heavy? Is it not a chemical composition of oxygen according to the periodic table of elements?"

Clemens, mesmerized by the tableau, manages distractedly to address her question, "Right you are, Eepia. Walt, do you care to elaborate with oratory? As I recall when I studied chemistry there were just a few known elements."

Disney admonishes Clemens, "Shhh. Listen to what they are saying. Quiet now and be reverent. This is a major event in the lives of these people."

Greene continues, "We have had the rare privilege of having had Hoss with us for these past 14 wonder-filled years, the best of my performing career. Why he was taken from us in that way, God himself only knows."

His voice is drowned out by Eepia's stage whisper, "Should I ask Gabriel at Heaven's Central Office about this, Mr. Disney?"

"No dear, just remain quiet and continue to listen."

Clemens removes his still unlit cigar from his mouth and tucks his spectacles in his white jacket; he continues to observe and witness the unfolding scene to discern what has already happened.

Lorne Greene asks, "Are there any last words from his actor-brothers before we begin shooting the third and final appearance of Samuel Clemens?" The cast and crew's voices drop to a murmur below the next conversation between Disney, Clemens, and Eepia.

"Did I jest hear my name mentioned? I do not recall being notified of such an occasion." Sam turns in some confusion to Disney and Eepia, "What does this all mean? Is this Hoss's untimely demise related to my own, when I was thought to've been prematurely ejected from my livelihood? I must say that my response to the newspaper in question was a worthy retraction, admirable in my estimation and not so exaggerated or overrated."

"Sam, please, I don't think it's about you this time, although why do you think there is a younger likeness of you with them?"

Clemens changes his focus, "If I do say so myself, not a spittin' image or likeness at all, 'cept for the moustache and hair. No, not one single bit. If I had my druthers, a better-fitting image would be the character I've seen from Heaven presuming my identity: Hal Holbrook seems to have a better vocabulary, much like mine, if I do say so. This young upstart is a poor imposter. He spouts off as an earlier version of myself. Why, in my day, he would have been run out of town on a rail for poor impersonations."

Eepia questions, "How can a person be run out on a rail? Is that a figure of speech?"

Disney responds quickly before Sam can utter another word, "Yes, Eepia. Being railroaded, or run out on a rail simply means he was hurriedly removed from the vicinity of a town on a locomotive, the fastest transportation at that time."

The Bonanza cast and crew intone "Amen" in unison, which stops our time travelers' dialog.

People pass tissues, use handkerchiefs, and hug one another for an extended time until the director announces, "OK, thank you, let's get this season underway. Time is money and later we'll address Dan's passing, but for now … ready on the set, take your places. Slate, scene 1, take 1 of year 14, episode 422."

The actors scatter, readying themselves, and take their places. "Lights, camera … action!"

Eepia is spellbound and holds tightly to the crystal sphere. She notices immediately as it reddens when Clemens approaches the actor portraying him; she gestures to caution him against it but Clemens turns back to her and quietly explains, "All I'm gonna do is coach him a bit on my cadence and delivery style. Is this not in keeping with why we are presumed to be present in this particular time?"

He casts his mind back to filming in 1909 at Stormfield in Connecticut, at the Clemens home, as if it were another of his stories for an audience.

I remember as if it were yesterday when Mr. Edison came to my home in Redding, it was the summer of '09. I was with my two daughters, Jean and Clara. First he took moving pictures of me inhaling one of my favorite stogies and walking in front of my home; not once, mind you, but twice, as if the first time was not good enough. Then he continued inside with the three of us—me being all prim and proper, sipping a foul mixture of watery manure reputed to be Ceylon tea—a most inhospitable drink, certainly not in keeping with my healthy style of living. I'd have liked to have changed one or two things about that, but if we are in the correct timeline now, that would not be possible.

He returns his attention to the present tableau and watches while the cameras are rolling. Clemens is fascinated by the film industry advancements and, as the opening scenes unfold, decides to add a touch or two. He steps into the scene with the actor who is portraying a younger version of himself. "Say there, young whippersnapper. To me, what you are expounding on is a total misstatement of the truth. I remember it distinctly, and I quote myself: 'the first 26 graves in Virginia City cemetery were occupied by murdered men'."

He points to the printed script in the youngster's hands. "That was me being modest while reporting back in the day. Try and iterate without a forked tongue, if you will." He looks about sheepishly, an impish grin blooming on his face, and continues, voice fading to nothing toward end of his speech, "As I recall, it was a time when I was camping nearby with some local dignitaries …"

The actor playing younger Clemens stutters, "Why, wh- who are you?"

The astounded director cuts in and, red-faced and angry, bellows through a megaphone, "Cut, CUT! I did not order, request, or wish to have an older impersonator duplicating Clemens. We'll have to reshoot. Take ten everyone and get this imposter off the set!"

By now the crystal is glowing bright red and emitting unusual, high-pitched sounds.

"Sam, do not interfere!" Gabriel suddenly warns, his voice gruff and disapproving, "This must play out according to plan, or else you will be removed for disrupting the time continuum. This is Walt's hour to view and review. He chose it deliberately. What part of that do you fail to understand? Do you so quickly forget what the sign in the dark room indicates?"

"OK, OK Gabe, don't get yourself in a tin Lizzy. I shall refrain from improving an oratory representing me—erroneously, I might add."

....

The ethereal image of recently deceased Dan Blocker, in his normal Hoss Cartwright costume, becomes visible only to Clemens, Disney, and Eepia. Blocker is obviously bewildered and perplexed when he is unable to communicate with anyone in the cast or crew.

A professional even now, he stays out of potential camera range, and an idea pops into his mind. The apparition moves to actor Victor Sen Yung who plays the Ponderosa's cook, Hop Sing, grabs his pigtails and ties them into a loose knot.

He whispers in Yung's ear, "Sorry Hop Sing, I've always wanted to do this. Take care of everyone and keep looking out for the family. You've been a good friend and I'll miss you."

The actors portraying Adam (Pernell Roberts), Little Joe (Michael Landon), and Pa (Lorne Greene) sense something is amiss. They turn quickly to Hop Sing as he yells excitedly, "Hoss here! Hop Sing feel him!" He points at his new hair style. "See?! He still at it, pull another prank!"

Adam, Little Joe, and Pa begin to giggle, then laugh harder, and finally guffaw at the sight as they recall Blocker's numerous pranks on the set. They finally wipe tears of bittersweet joy from their eyes and smile.

Yung sighs, shrugs his shoulders, content to be the brunt of the joke. The entire crew dissolves into laughter and giggling, which helps to lighten the atmosphere.

....

"Mr. Clemens, please!" Eepia admonishes him, "You are endangering our trip through time. Please stop immediately, any further disruptions may result in, in … "

Clemens ignores her and declares to younger actor, "Young man, as I recall, it goes like this …" Clemens continues to explain, and the actor's face glows in total amazement. Around them, overhead lights blaze, and people scatter and scramble about on the set; it's near pandemonium before they can reset and reshoot the scene.

"… and that's how I see it," Clemens concludes. "Do you understand better now?"

The director is practically apoplectic. His face is an ashen purple. He yells, "Remove that imposter now!"

The young Clemens actor is engrossed in listening to Sam, "Yes, I think I do. Mister, whoever you are, I am much obliged and appreciate your valuable input into my characterization. Thank you, I'm much obliged."

"You are certainly welcome, young man, 'tweren't nuthin', nuthin' at all." Clemens looks at the actor portraying his younger self, pulls a candy bar from inside his jacket, unwraps it and takes a bite. Irrepressible, he pulls out a pen and autographs the wrapper with his nom de plume, just as he had before.

The crystal is pulsating bright crimson light and emitting a squealing, ethereal sound unlike anything heard on earth. Eepia is truly alarmed, "The crystal seems about to explode. This timeline is nearly severed; we are causing insurmountable damage. Take my hand, we leave immediately."

Disney declares, "Now you've done it Sam! I feel a strong tingle commencing …" Holding on to one another, they gradually dissolve into nothingness while the set is a roiling mass of almost hysterical people milling about in complete confusion, unable to continue with the scene.

Disney knows he has pulled one over on his mentor but is also unnerved. His prank has had an unintended consequence he'll have to address with the heavenly hierarchy.

The distraught director's face is livid and he yells through the megaphone, "All right, all right already! I've had and seen enough. Today I'm done! Come back tomorrow, or ... no, make it two days, then let's see if we can do it right next time, without any more fake Twains."

Clemens hears him even as he is dematerializing and takes umbrage, "Humph; he's got some nerve callin' me an imposter!"

Disney placates him, "My, my, did we get your dander up?"

"Out of spite, if I thought it would do any good, I'd return tomorrow, just to give him a piece of my mind. What do you think about that Walt?"

"No! Your mind has risen above a few bumps and bruises along the way, long before me. I think it's OK the way it is. Besides, let me check something," He reaches into one of his pockets and brings out a fashionable chronometer, "I'm certain this wasn't a complete hour yet."

He looks towards the swirling light purple mass of Eepia, now dressed in a Western-cut leather skirt, white high collar frilly blouse and walking boots with engraved flowers. She answers, "Mr. Disney, yes, there is still a little time left before the hour is up. What have you in mind?"

Disney pauses for a moment, thinking aloud, "There is someone I'd like to see. I caught a glimpse of his energetic vitality from my viewing goggles before venturing on this journey of exploration. Yes, let's go there...."

Back on the Ponderosa set, unnoticed by anyone, a lone cameraman has captured the unusual episode and aftermath on his personal 8mm camera. He tucks it away carefully before readying his equipment for another day, whistling absentmindedly, "Whistle While You Work."

∞

CHAPTER 8

Menlo Park, CA, circa 1973

ANGRY-LOOKING clouds hide the brilliance of the sun. The travelers reappear in a sleepy suburban neighborhood. A garage sale is in progress at the house before them; various items are laid out on the driveway and on the yellowed grass of an unkempt yard, each bearing stickers declaring their potential price.

"Say, what have we here?" Disney exclaims, "I didn't set my noggin for this—looks like a garage sale. Interesting turn of events, I don't remember the last time I attended one."

"What this looks like to me," Clemens comments in his unedited superfluous style, "is the decluttering of a carriage house from un-useful junk."

"That's right, Sam, in your day there were hardly any automobiles to speak of, only horses with their carriages and such. This may have been known to you as a …" he deliberately counts these on his fingers, "Yard sale, rummage sale, tag sale, lawn sale, attic sale, moving sale, garage sale, thrift sale, or junk sale. Take your pick. It's an informal, irregularly scheduled event on one's own premises, where private individuals sell their used goods. Typically, the goods in a garage sale are unwanted by the homeowners."

Disney is giddy to be able to outspeak his mentor for once. "As you can tell, some of the items on display are like new. They are for sale because the owner neither wants nor needs them, or wants to minimize his possessions, or to raise funds. He looks around and announces, "It appears the young lads inside the garage are the proprietors of this menagerie."

"That's a bit flippant, don't you think, Walt?"

"Oh, pardon my choice of words. After all you are the wordsmith, I'm just an imagineer." Disney moves about, checking the prices of a few things lying about.

"As I recall," Clemens comments, "some people with literary brains thought of me as an 'unpolished diamond,' even called me a man whose crusty diatribes had deep moral and humanitarian roots. Maybe some of my critics were a bit perceptive after all."

Eepia looks around, fascinated by all the tools, equipment, pots and pans, and other household paraphernalia. "Are these not supposed to be inside the big building? They will surely rust if the clouds begin watering, is that not so?"

Disney chuckles indulgently under his breath, "No dear, these items are no longer useful to the occupants and they are being sold at a fraction of their original cost, hence the reason for their outside display."

"Eepia confused, the garage is not for sale? And if it is, maybe that is the reason all this other stuff is outside, soon to gather moisture from the dark clouds above?"

Clemens snickers, "Eepia, that is an astute observation for a newbie, I must say."

Disney shakes his head, forcing himself not to laugh at her naiveté. "Eepia, such a sale is a custom these days. When items are no longer needed, the property owners post a sign outside their homes and advertise. Anyone who comes by can look and decide if they want what the household no longer needs."

"Oh, I see," Clemens affirms, "they throw out their trash for someone to peruse and, liking it, secure it by means of monetary exchange: trash for another's treasure, a more practical solution." From a nearby table, he picks up an avocado green waffle maker with an electrical cord and plug. "And what do we call this contraption?"

"A waffle maker." Walt laughs. "Instead of pancakes, this is used to make waffles. Have you ever tried one?"

"It looks like a hose has been attached to it—for what useful purpose?" Clemens doesn't bother to wait for an answer. "In my day, I would use a flap-jack griddle. The modern, improved design of this consarned apparatus still has those little squares, makes sense to me to fill 'em with some maple syrup; that I do take notice of … mmmm. My stomach is thinkin' about digesting my backbone."

He looks about for their crystal monitor, "Eepia, where is the nearest eatery? Can you look it up with that crystal apparatus?"

Eepia has noticed a tree down the block and across the street and has not paid attention to Sam's request because, as she watches raptly, several objects fall from the branches to the ground. Curiosity drives her and impulse takes over; she must see more. Still wearing Western clothing, she crosses the street quickly, not checking for any oncoming cars. Fortunately, there is no traffic in the neighborhood. Reaching the tree, she eagerly bends down and picks up several red, ripe, delicious-looking apples that have dropped.

She returns to her companions, still not knowing to look for oncoming vehicles, and hands one to Clemens. "Eepia think this help with your backbone?"

He laughs heartily and graciously accepts it, although carefully inspects it first for worms. Finding none, he takes a bite. "Delicious! Much obliged Eve, err, Eepia. Is this from across the street or Paradise?"

"Paradise," she points upward, "is that a term for a place across the street too? These I found for you but did not want to disturb the ones that were still attached. Did I do something wrong, is that not acceptable? And why did you call me Eve? Is it not still daylight?"

"Paradise is a biblical reference, dearie, and so is the reference to the name Eve, not to be confused with the term evening, as you may have thought."

"Oh, Eepia see correctly now. Thank you, Mr. Clemens."

Disney has been checking through numerous sale items and stops to comment. "Eepia, the term would be to see clearly, however you are also correct by seeing correctly, see?"

"Language is confusing. Eepia trying harder to understand."

Disney turns to look at Clemens still munching on the apple. "Didn't you allude in one of your writings to something about biblical speeches and unconscious plagiarism?"

He beams delightedly at the remembrance, "Yes, as a matter of fact I do. I was on a vacation to the Cook Islands in the Pacific. You now refer to them as Hawaiian Islands."

"Yes, we do. Go on, as if you need any urging from anyone here."

Clemens takes a deep, all-consuming breath while moving absentmindedly among the displays, "Livvy and I were on a vacation long ago, and we decided to spend a Sunday morning reaffirming my Christian upbringing at a Southern Baptist church nearby. After quite the fiery sermon I conversed with the minister. I informed him that his sermon was most engaging and eloquent and inquired if he had ever heard of unconscious plagiarism?"

He pauses for a response from Disney, who stands attentive but mute.

Eepia is listening intently, trying to keep up with the yarn Clemens spins in front of her.

"Anyway, the minister looked blankly at me and said he did not. I explained that unconscious plagiarism is when someone quotes text word for word that was written before and, if he would like, when I returned home I would send him the exact quotations in question."

"How did the minister take it?"

"He was much obliged with my keen sense of the word and said he would be looking forward to what I might send him as elucidation about his so-called plagiarism."

Disney wishes now he hadn't started Sam down this narrative path. Resigned, he asks, "And how did that turn out, might I ask?"

Sam's eyes sparkle with glee, "When we returned home to Hannibal, I looked it up and sure enough, there it was, word for word, so I bundled it up and sent it off to him directly."

"Did you keep a copy for yourself?"

Clemens rocks back and forth on his heels, readying himself for the self-satisfying punchline, holding their gazes. "Yes, I most assuredly did."

"Where in Heaven's name did you find such a resource back then?

"I sent him one of the Bibles I had on hand."

Disney's face is blank until it registers. The Bible! His chortles escalate to guffaws.

Eepia giggles too, not comprehending why Disney is laughing so uproariously. In her usual learning mode, she says, "I still not understand but it seem funny anyway."

Clemens succumbs to a full horselaugh, slapping his knee at his successful jocularity.

Disney turns back to Eepia after wiping tears from his eyes, still rumbling with laughter, "Eepia, do I not get one of your apples from across the street too?"

"Your backbone fine. But your eyes watering. I worry ..."

She points out, "Mr. Disney seem in pain. Would you like one? I can get. Would that help your eyes from watering?"

Clemens erupts afresh in laughter, barely catching his breath, "Eepia, you slay me, girl!"

Disney's sides are hurting from so much laughing, but he slowly calms down and assures her, "No, that is quite all right. You have done enough already. Take a look around and see if you find anything that interests you, either on a tabletop or the ground, OK?"

....

Young-adult Steve Jobs stands at a large table inside the garage; he excuses himself from his two housemates and ambles outside to see if the three customers outside might buy something. Waving his arms to encompass the sale items, he inquires, "Can I help you? Do you see anything you want, or maybe need? My two friends and I are raising capital to launch our project, a home computer."

Disney looks at him, intrigued, "A home computer? Interesting concept. The ones I've seen would take up most of that garage space you have back there, and then some. Are you trying to make it smaller—not the garage, but a computer—for home use you say?"

Eepia understands Disney is using precise language to avoid confusing her any more than necessary ... most considerate of him.

That's my point exactly," Jobs answers. "As it is, a computer takes up too much space and is not viable for consumer use. We're going to change the dynamics of computing for all time. We're just a bit short of funds, so we decided to have this garage sale to supplement our current cash flow."

Clemens, rummaging through the many utensils, tools, and outmoded appliances on a table, holds up a hand mixer. "I never would have thought that a pair of egg beaters would no longer be of value. The chickens themselves might have had to cast a vote or two at least. According to my sources they always thought better of that."

Eepia takes the master wordsmith's bait again, "You talked with chickens?"

"I always tried to cackle a word or two with the best of them. Sometimes I would sit in the henhouse … that was when there was no dog house. Livvy had a temper at times. I found them to have a certain ripe odoriferousness. The rooster would look me in the eye and cock his head before challenging me. But I just blew smoke from my cigar and that usually did the trick. He would leave me be to roost for myself."

"You are blowing proverbial smoke again, Sam," Disney remarks. "Eepia takes all you say in literally, or haven't you noticed?"

Stunned by Walt's disclosure, Clemens retorts, "I've been minding my P's and Q's, if you know what I mean."

Clemens takes one bite from another apple and, on sudden impulse, offers it to Jobs. "My young lad, this here apple is for your use; maybe you can do something with it as well, if for no other reason than to look at it with wonderment. Who knows, something might just come of it; might be something marketable." He looks around and shrugs his shoulders, "I do not see anything else of value at this time. You can sell the garage if need be. I'm certain the horse wouldn't mind, seein' as you don't have any to spare."

He winks and saunters off down the street, self-satisfied, and Eepia follows silently. Disney stays behind for the moment, "Well youngster, good luck to you. Maybe we'll see you again sometime. And good luck, too, with fitting a computer into a smaller box; maybe it will be more useful that way, for anyone who has a mind to use one." He trails after his traveling companions.

Jobs turns to return to the garage, then looks back at the three, mumbling, "I think I know the older man all dressed in white from somewhere. The other one, it's his voice that's familiar. Not the young lady—definitely I'd remember her."

He glances quizzically at the apple in his hand, wondering why someone would hand him an apple with a large bite taken from it.

The lightbulb of inspiration flashes.

He trots back toward his two partners, waving the apple back and forth at them. As Jobs re-enters the garage, "Say guys, you're not going to believe this."

They stop what they were doing.

Steve Wozniak responds, "What's up?"

"We just had a visit from a white- haired geezer, who I think looked like Samuel Clemens himself, you know, Mark Twain, writer and author of required fifth or sixth grade reading, Tom Sawyer, ... and I know that's not possible."

"And?"

"And the younger man with him—there was something about his voice. I could swear it was Walt Disney's voice. Am I going crazy?"

"Whoa. Well, it could also be because you haven't slept for the last 36 hours or so; could be a hallucination."

Third partner Ron Wayne comments without sarcasm, "Definitely not because of inhalants, that's for certain."

Jobs is clearly excited and continues, holding up the apple again, "Yes, but look what the old guy gave me and told me to think about making a marketable product with it."

The three look in surprise at the piece of fruit in Jobs' hand. Recognition dawns.

....

Clemens, Disney, and Eepia continue walking away from the garage sale. They pass under the apple tree and stop to gather one or two for later, to Eepia's obvious pleasure. Clemens remarks offhandedly, "Do you know I have a few patents?"

Disney does, and sees an opportunity. "I seem to remember a journal article about your vest strap: you were referred to as 'an inventor, not a great one but one of those who dream of making a fortune from some bright idea and never quite achieve it, except perhaps in a modest manner.' Is that about right?"

Sam is slightly miffed, "I more than recall it; it was an interference from Mr. Lockwood." He speaks under his breath, "the dunderhead," then continues at full volume. "But it was useful for my utilization of words on paper; I did receive the patent after I wrote the Patent office a story about my elastic strap. No more need be said about it, except for the other two patents during my lifetime—one for a self-pasting scrapbook (No. 140,245) granted in 1873, which proved quite commercially profitable. And another for a game to make it easier for players to remember historical dates (No. 324,535), should you need verification of my veracity."

Munching on yet another apple, Sam inquires, "Did you get any patents?"

Disney smirks with false modesty, "Yes, for the multiplane camera used for animation, after I created my mouse, Mickey. And there may have been a few more registered in my name."

The men progressively dissolve into nothingness as they continue walking. Eepia skips joyfully along in the moment before realizing they are nearly dematerialized, "Oh, wait, wait for me..."

∞

CHAPTER 9

A Feisty Bank Heist?

$\mathcal{P}$ATRONS are lying on the cold tile floor, frozen with fear, inside a well-known national banking institution. A deranged, wild-eyed paranoid young man waves a Colt M1911, threatening everyone.

Clemens, Disney, and Eepia suddenly materialize right in front of him, startling him so badly he discharges a shot into the ceiling and dispels any doubt that the pistol has real bullets in it!

Numerous people on the floor cringe and a few whimper, believing this could be one of the last moments of their lives, and a couple of the women begin to wail uncontrollably, which freaks out the men. A female customer still standing close to a marble pillar is completely petrified. Although she is near a wall phone hanging behind the nearby pillar, she is much too scared to do anything with it.

Eepia is still in western-style clothing but now cocks her head to one side and innocently studies the standing woman, who is dressed in a polyester pantsuit and a white ruffled blouse, her hair in a blonde pageboy.

Eepia rapidly morphs into an identical image; she has found her new role model.

Shaking off the sudden interruption, the young bank robber yells at them in a high-pitched, alarmingly loud voice, "All right you three, reach for the sky!"

Eepia stares at the man, analyzing his demand, then slowly stretches her arms high above her head; her body floats upward. Glancing at her sidelong, Disney sighs impatiently and points insistently for her to plant herself back on the floor. Confused, she floats back to his side. "Is this what that man with a gun wants?"

The robber is stunned and momentarily at a loss for words.

Disney mutters under his breath, "This is going to be quite interesting."

"You find a dunderhead with a gun of some interest?" Clemens is amazed, definitely not amused.

Disney nods, chuckling to himself at the irony.

The robber has struggled to regain some composure and points the gun directly at Eepia. "All right lady, you've gone and made me mad now. Hit the floor!!"

She tries very hard to please him. Insecurity and innocence radiating through her demeanor, she buckles at the knees, bends down, and firmly smacks the floor with her hands three times.

Clemens and Disney can't control their grins as she complies so literally.

The robber is clearly unnerved by her, "I can't believe this!"

"Walt," Clemens utters under his breath, "is this still holdin' your amusement?"

With a knowing and humor-filled grin, Disney answer, "Certainly is."

"May a fragile old man inquire as to the source of your amusement?"

"This young man has the audacity to be threatening us with a gun."

"It is my considered opinion that this is not a good time for a narrative, Walt! Our very lives are in danger."

Disney smiles broadly, "Really, Sam? How do you figure that?"

"If you are trying to be brave, may I tell you that few things are harder to put up with than the annoyance of a good example?"

"Be objective, my friend. Examine the situation we've found ourselves in."

Clemens eyes suddenly sparkle in realization, "Oh. Do you suppose he could damage us in any way at all? What are our limitations here?"

"I don't know. Interesting, isn't it?" Disney turns to Eepia, "Can you enlighten us?"

She has been admiring her new image in a tall mirror. Still attentive to Disney, she moves the crystal to her forehead obediently. "Market Street Bank, April 29, 1977, Omaha, Nebraska; time, 12:33 p.m. Youth holds 17 people hostage. Demands money and rides out of the city."

The robber counts those on the floor and is stunned at her accuracy, plus he has just watched this woman change her entire wardrobe and hair style in a heartbeat, take him at his word, and then top it off by putting a weird crystal to her forehead and reciting details. "Shuddup! Ugh, this is so creepy!! I have had about all that I can take from you three! Do like the others! Lie down on the floor … now!!"

Clemens is quick, "Don't do it, Eepia! All we need is for you to curl up for a nap."

Disney chuckles and he and Clemens slowly comply, lying down on the floor and propped up on their elbows. Eepia is thoroughly distracted by her new look and goes back to admiring her reflection in the nearby mirror. She slowly turns to see all the angles.

The many patrons remain motionless, their foreheads against the cold tile floor, unaware of what is transpiring. The pant-suited woman slides down the pillar and spreads out on the floor as the young robber demanded. The telephone was so near; it's completely out of reach now.

"Sam," Disney realizes, "I am suddenly aware of how shackled we human beings have been by the fear of death. It has been blackmailing our initiative since the beginning of reason."

Clemens turns on his side to face him. Utter disbelief colors his voice, "Walt, now is not the time to indulge in philosophical diatribes. We must address this situation. This man has some enormously foul personal habits. You know that nothing so needs reforming as other people's habits, right?"

"I'm serious." Disney feels real fear, which he has not felt for a very long time. Sweat begins to bead on his forehead. "Look at us! Here we are all following the orders of a mightily disturbed young man just because he is manipulating our fear of death."

The robber threatens them with the gun and growls, "I'll show you death. If you say even one more word…"

Clemens deliberately ignores the man, far more interested in his own opinion. "Never thought about how stifled folks have been through history for that very reason. I do have to wonder how vulnerable we really are, though … I mean, if you pricked my hand, would it bleed now?"

His eyes dance impishly and he slowly turns toward Eepia. "Here, Eepia dear, give Uncle Sam your hand."

Eepia turns and holds out her hand innocently.

Disney intervenes with a scolding look, shakes a finger at Clemens and stops her just in time. He motions for Eepia to go back to looking in the mirror. "As I was saying, death is the one subject that scares the human race so deeply they simply block it out of their minds."

"I once said and still hold to that way of thinkin', people are sorely confused. They celebrate birth and mourn death, but only because they aren't the person involved."

"I don't agree. Both hold a beauty and are equally wonderful. But that fear underlies every decision we make, consciously or not."

The robber doesn't know quite what to do at this point; he's undercut by their actions and philosophical conversation, and stunned because they are not paying any attention to him. He holds his ground but feels drawn to attend to their dialog.

Clemens is enjoying the discourse, "True. We all tried to be supremely honorable and good because of that fear. I learned something important: be good and you will most certainly be lonesome."

"By the way Sam, have you ever been serious?"

"I get so carried away with being entertaining I don't know if I can tell the difference."

"Answer me this, then: did you ever feel guilty when someone died?"

Clemens is abruptly thoughtful and sad, "Yes, three times. My firstborn, Langdon, died at 19 months, then my daughter Susie, and lastly when Olivia…" He sighs audibly, "My beloved wife Livvy died too. I felt I'd failed them. I was totally consumed by bitterness and guilt, believing I was the cause of their pain and lack in their lives. Yes, I know guilt."

The young robber, clearly unnerved by his lack of power over this trio, has lost track of what he came here to do. He helplessly watches Clemens and Disney as they persist in talking, undisturbed by the situation around them.

Eepia continues to pivot, studying herself in the mirror. Her reflection has her full attention.

The robber comments, "You know … when my grandma died I felt responsible. It was terrible." He's not speaking to anyone in particular and leans against a stained glass partition, remembering. "She was the only person in this world who really loved me. She really did, ya know? My folks never wanted me, but she did. I never let her know that it counted."

Disney and Clemens have heard him and gaze at the young man with compassion. Walt understands, "Grandmothers know things like that. You didn't have to say it aloud. She understood you, I'm sure of it. "

Now teary eyed, the robber relaxes the Colt's angle toward the floor. "I came home from school. She was lying on the kitchen floor. I yelled at her not to be dead. I hadn't done the chores that the morning … she begged me to, as usual, and I just ran on to school." He chokes out a sob, "and then she died."

Eepia finally drags her attention away from herself toward the lad holding the pistol and wails, "Please, do not be sad, boy. You are not alone. Mr. Clemens will give you a candy bar to eat with your hands, but you must take paper off first."

Clemens sarcastically challenges the young robber, "He'll have to shoot me for it."

The crystal is flashing warning red pulses in Eepia's hand. Disney coughs, a trademark response, and remarks, "Look at the control we have. Nothing to fear from anything. Death has no hold on us. I could simply walk over and take the gun from him."

Clemens is astonished with Walt's audacity, "Are you a little inebriated with power?"

Eepia firmly reacts, "No! Crystal say we not change events!"

The robber is in a quandary, "I - I don't understand, what's happening? What is she yapping about? "

Disney is protectively adamant, as if these people are all his extended family, "We're just supposed to let this robbery happen? What if someone gets hurt?"

Sam thoughtfully suggests, "Would you listen to yourself? You're a total contradiction. You know life is an ongoing eternal process and here you go getting caught up in his play, this Shakespearean performance of life."

"You're absolutely right. It's amazingly easy to fall for the old metaphor. It's a habitual train of thought. All of these people—no matter what, their souls are fine."

Eepia gasps firmly, "Mr. Disney, please, do not interfere with the time-line. Remember the last time you did, at that concert?"

Clemens winks at them and ambles to a nearby writing table. He picks up a ballpoint pen chained to the marble top. Laughing, he points to the pen and shakes his head, "Human is the only animal who would think to chain up a writing implement … or who would need to."

Taking a deposit slip from a rack, he signs, "My very best to you and yours, fondly Mark Twain." With a sly smirk, he walks over to the robber and tucks it into his shirt pocket. "This oughta confuse 'em."

The crystal glows a solid crimson, pulsating rhythmically, and now emitting a foghorn-like bellowing sound only the three can hear.

Sparkles surround them, signaling immediate transference

The robber feels faint. This is so odd! He reaches weakly for the paper in his pocket.

"Something's wrong here." Disney is now alarmed, "It hasn't been any-where near the allotted hour."

Angel Gabriel's heavenly voice bellows loud and clear in the travelers' ears, "We terminate each visit when either of you interferes with the time flow of the past. Samuel, you know better than to sign that paper. Eepia, get over there. We must move you on to a new time. Walt, choose it now!"

Clemens looks anything but sorry and an impish smile teases at the cor-ners of his mouth.

Eepia leaves the mirrored pillar and draws nearer as instructed. She searches for a pocket to tuck the crystal into, but her current wardrobe has none. The threesome begins to dissolve in a swirling, colorful vortex.

The robber gapes in utter confusion; his original thought had been 'this is gonna be an easy cash advance' but, between his gun being loaded with real bullets, the paper the old guy left for him, the still-frozen bank patrons on the floor, the dematerializing images of Disney, Eepia, and Clemens, and a deep, penetrating voice coming out of nowhere, he is utterly paralyzed.

Disney shouts, "One thing, Sir … we couldn't have been harmed in any way by that weapon, right?"

"While you are on earth, you are wholly mortal." The Heavenly Voice adds, "Along with this opportunity you must accept mortal vulnerabilities."

Clemens is shocked; his eyes flash angrily at Disney, "Dunderhead!!"

The robber is discombobulated; our travelers never know what he decided to do—or not.

....

They are in the void. As they prepare for the next educational advancement through time, Walt reviews their amazing conscious journey. "So far, Sam, you've overutilized your writing talents more than three times their allotment, which was zero to begin with. You are supposed to be a mentor and tutor to Eepia—part of your reason for going along with me, remember Gabriel's comment after our first joint lesson of togetherness? You have managed to upset things more than once...."

Sam cuts in, "And you've had your fun with the near-spittin' image of me at that western abode inside a cavernous building, somewhere in a metropolitan area."

It's Eepia's turn to contribute. "Like my outfit? Does it fit with the theme? And my new hairdo, should I change it?" She realizes they are not interested in her physical investment in clothing, hair style, and accessories; she decides instead to disrobe.

"Eepia, for Pete's sake, keep yer clothes on." Disney is adamant and embarrassed, "This is no time for you to change without being properly ensconced in a more private setting. You are with two adults and we are not accustomed to seeing you change, especially in this way."

"Walt's right," Sam exclaims, revealing a shred of humanness, parental understanding and control, "Maybe I've been a bit lacking in my tutoring and such about proper etiquette and decorum. I shall endeavor to be more attentive, so please be more careful when you're around adults when decidin' to change appearances. The next time could prove to be less than satisfactory."

Gabriel's voice interposes, "Yes, Eepia, remember, as a new soul, your duty is to listen to these two and learn what you may, sometimes despite some of their actions and discussions, OK?"

She understands the admonishment and, dissuaded by all their spontaneous reactions, quickly straightens her clothing, "Eepia sorry, I'm not used to having to behave any differently as I was not used to costuming myself at all where I came from. Since this is my first time in this form it is befuddling, trying, and stressing me out!"

"Oh my gawd, Sam, she's becoming a teenager!"

"And far too soon to suit my good-tempered nature."

"Your good-tempered nature, Sam? Who are you really? Did you somehow switch personalities with that younger version of yourself—all without my notice—just so you could get back at me for my little practical joke?"

"Enough already!" Gabriel's voice exclaims, "Time is getting short, Walt, and you've yet to decide where the next adventure lands you."

Walt grins at the appropriate hint of where they might go next, "Thanks for the forethought Gabriel, and away we go...."

∞

CHAPTER *10*

Los Angeles Olympics, 1984

$STARS$ are still clearly visible, although dawn's light glows on the eastern horizon. A lone runner is carrying a blazing Olympic torch past unbroken lines of barbed wire fencing.

A horse whinnies and a dog barks, as if responding to the runner's footfalls.

Elsewhere it is quiet.

Clemens and Eepia appear to one side of the runner, but Disney materializes directly in front of him. There is no time for the torchbearer to make evasive moves to avoid a collision.

They tumble hard.

Somehow, the torch stays lit, and the runner tosses it to Clemens before he surveys the damage. The astonished old gentleman protests, "What in the wide world is this in my hands for? What are you doing out here, son?"

"I'm … an Olympic runner … that's the Olympic torch, it's been carried by many short-distance runners all the way from Greece. It has to keep going. Where did you come from? I can see clearly for two or three miles and you just appeared! I swear it!"

Eepia utters, "Yes, it's true. We just appeared in front of you. We are from Heaven. We are—"

Clemens and Disney both panic. Disney steps in to redirect the conversation and asks, as he helps him up, "Are you hurt?"

Clemens follows suit, "What's your name, son?"

"I'm Rex McDougal." He grimaces, "I think I've injured my right knee pretty badly."

Disney, always quick to step in, "Let's get you some help." He scans the dawn horizon and sees a light on in the near distance. "I think there's a farmhouse over there. I'll try to get them to get us to a doctor."

Rex is in pain but adamant, "Wait! This torch must get to the next runner first and foremost! We are on a very tight schedule and we have to get on with it right now. It's only a mile or so more down the road."

Eepia will help you, Rex. I will get it to the next person. Someone must hold the crystal while I do it, though."

The crystal blares a bright red color as she tries to hand it to Clemens. He backs away.

"I'm sorry, Mr. Clemens, it doesn't trust you."

"Hmmm, I'm not so taken with it, either."

"Don't pout, Sam. You must be the bearer of the Olympic torch." Disney clutches his leg, faking pain, "I am in no condition to carry it, see?"

"Is this the same idea as in ancient times?" Clemens is clearly not amused. "Am I going to have to wrap myself in a linen diaper and run in sandals? If that is the case, you can most certainly douse this flame."

Rex is anguished, both by pain and Sam's suggestion, and insists, "You're just fine, old man. Just keep going until you meet another runner. Please! It's vital!"

Clemens feels put out by the words, old man.

Always questioning. Disney needs to know, "Where are we, when are we? This must be an Olympic year."

The runner winces again and the naïve comment surprises him. "The '84 Olympics are being held in Los Angeles, and we are getting so close. We must get the torch to the Coliseum by tomorrow, and in time." He looks askance, "How could you not know?"

Disney pretends it all is coming back to him and nods. "Of course, just down the road, Los Angles, the Coliseum, 1984."

"I will go with Mr. Clemens," Eepia volunteers, "unless there is something against it. Hurry, let's run."

Clemens stares deeply into Disney's face before moving away with the torch. Its flame flickers. Surely the ridiculousness of the situation would be obvious to his friend! Clemens addresses his companions with as much sarcasm as he can muster, "Oh yes, Eepia. You and I will run at maximum speed, carrying this stick with a blazing fire atop it. The reason my head is atilt is that any minute now my friend is going to be hit with a mighty dose of reason and his escapade will end abruptly."

Disney is engrossed with a way to aid the injured runner. He waves them along. "NO, I've got this, you two need to go now, as Rex says."

Clemens is irked, and huffs off down the road. Grumbling all the way.

Eepia is delighted. "Oh look, a pink sky crystal!"

"You look. I'm busy." Totally disgruntled he looks nonetheless, and retorts, "That's a star, not a crystal. The pink stuff is the sky."

"Still, so pretty."

"Don't you ever come down from that cloud? It's cold. It's early. My shoes hurt my wholly mortal feet. I am not enjoying this one iota."

"You, Mr. Clemens, are used to the beauty and the smells and the sounds here on earth. I never knew things could feel so nice. My face just smiles on its own, the more I see and hear and feel." She sees his ill-tempered smirk, "I am not trying to make you angry."

"Good. Let's not talk about this wonderful experience then. Is this a side trip or sumthin'? Any thoughts about why?"

They continue at a slow pace with Eepia urging him almost continuously to move a little faster. She holds up the crystal to her forehead, "I have no answer from the crystal. Do you have another thought?"

"Yes, as a matter of fact! I am tired, and my arm is sore. S'pose we could put this thing out and not have to carry it at such an arc until we see some-one ... and then we could light it?"

"No! It must stay lit." Eepia is horrified, "Please be honest, Mr. Clemens."

A sly grin grows on his lips, "I was just testing your honesty. I had no intention of putting it out."

"That's an untruth and you know it." She gives him a stern look.

"There are several good protections against temptations, but the surest two are cowardice and the company of a new soul."

Eepia still demonstrates her naivete, "Thank you, I think."

Clemens is reaching the end of his physical limits. Half walking and half resting, he shuffles down the road while Eepia bounces perkily at his side, silently humming to herself.

....

A modified Harley-Davidson Model U with an Art Deco-trimmed side car approaches and the greasy-looking driver is showing off for his girlfriend as she sits alongside. They slow down and the biker remarks, "Kind of an old dude to be makin' the trek, aren't ya?"

Clemens quips back shortly, "It wasn't my original plan to be out here."

"I suppose you were drafted because of your good physique? Hey old duffer, you belong in a home, a rest home that is." The girlfriend slaps her partner's back for his snide cleverness and laughs.

Irked, Clemens stops dead in his tracks.

Eepia doesn't quite know what to do and she's not prepared to say any-thing. She stands silently and watches their every move.

The biker shuts off the motor and puts his foot down to balance the bike. He leers at Clemens, who holds his head high, unwavering.

Still angry, Sam says, "Eepia, there is a lesson to be learned here. Let's be grateful for the fools. But for these folks, the rest of us would not look so bright."

"Mr. Clemens, let's not be brave now. I'm scared of this dunderhead. Let's run."

Run? What on god's green earth do you think I've been doin' anyway, sleep walking?"

The biker dismounts and slaps his fist into his palm menacingly as he walks toward Clemens. "Who you callin' a fool?"

"Aw, shucks," Clemens is quick to retort, a bit surprised the biker understood, "I had looked forward to handling this situation solo, but unfortunately my friends are coming down the roadway here with reinforcements." He sports a sly magnanimous grin, "look up that-a-way if you care to, or can you see that far?"

....

Back up the road, Disney, the runner, and several other people are quickly closing the gap between them.

Eepia watches the biker retreat to his Harley and release the kickstand in a move to escape a larger confrontation.

Eepia sighs, "Mr. Clemens, you are the bravest man in the world. I was so scared, but you were not."

"Always remember this. Courage is not resistance to fear, but the mastery of fear—not its absence."

"Yes, thank you for the lesson; I will try to make better sense of it."

Disney catches up with a small group of onlookers cheering Clemens for saving the torch. The torchbearer is ready to resume his run. "Rex is ready, Sam. We've bandaged his leg and he wants to continue. Is that OK with you, or would you like to carry the torch for a little longer?"

Clemens is suddenly morose and reminisces, "First time I carried a torch was for Livvy. This one has been an afterthought, not the same in any way, shape, or form." He slowly relinquishes the torch to Rex, who continues down the road. A small cadre of Olympics fans applauds as he passes by each one.

Walt nods to Sam, grins, and points to the biker who is having trouble starting his Harley. Clemens motions for Eepia to follow and stands directly in front of the biker and his biker chick.

The crystal immediately glares crimson … again.

Clemens grabs a pen from his pocket and reaches into his jacket for a candy bar, all the while never taking his eyes off the biker's face. "You are a person who thinks he has all the answers. Am I right?"

"More than you have, old man, that's fer sure!"

"That so? Here, I want you to have a memento, and I want to hear your answer for what is about to happen. Years from now, when you think about the next few seconds, it might be helpful to realize it would never have happened had you been a little less ignorant."

Confused, but not doubting his control, the biker confidently smirks at his girlfriend in imagined superiority. She smiles back, her mouth missing several front teeth.

"Whatcha got for me, old man? Not yer clothes, I hope; musta been stolen from an unconscious Good Humor man, or maybe Colonel Sanders ... whaddya think?"

The lady biker reaches up and slaps her partner on the shoulder, laughing much too loudly at his nasty remark.

Commandingly, Clemens says, "Watch ... me ... very carefully. Have a candy bar..."

The biker slowly takes the autographed candy bar and is abruptly stupefied to see Disney, Clemens, and Eepia simply dissolve into thin air right in front of him. Breathless and light-headed, he sees the words scribbled on the candy wrapper:

When angry, count to four. When very angry, swear. Fondly, Mark Twain ... yes, it is I.

....

They are in the void again. Walt is digesting these most recent events and noticing Sam has been more attentive toward Eepia, even remorseful about a few of his antics. His warmth toward his ingenuous protégé has been slowly evolving from previous dismissive behavioral traits and disgruntled claims of ineptitude to one of growing up into a responsive female with her own thoughts.

"You know Sam, I sense you've been pretty good with entertaining us and how you're handling of our newbie. She responds to how you have been acting toward her."

"A bit more fatherly like than I'd like to admit. She has tender to get under my skin."

"How can I get under your skin, Mr. Clemens? That seems utterly impossible, I might add."

"It's just another one of his quirks, Eepia, using language to befuddle even a literate person. Sam, I understand your inventive propensity for autographing candy wrappers, and in this case it may have been even called for. Still, that sort of thing can certainly backfire." Walt snickers at the thought of the biker's face as they disintegrated.

Gabriel chimes in, "I witnessed your most recent and regrettable shenigans. This one requires a more intense investigation into what happens next to that biker and his companion. I'll get back to you on this..." His voice trails off into the void.

Disney is concerned but decides to be silent as they move to the next stop in their adventure. He impulsively decides to return somewhere they had already visited.

Sam makes a final pronouncement, "Well, he deserved it and his mistress was just as guilty for playing into that foul mouth's hand. Humph!"

Eepia is a bit distraught at being unable to stem Clemens' impetuousness but says nothing.

∞

CHAPTER *11*

Disneyworld Florida, 1986

DISNEY, Clemens, and Eepia materialize at the Experimental Prototype Community of Tomorrow (EPCOT) Center one at a time. Eepia is the last to arrive. They find themselves in a large suite inside a huge sphere that, from the outside, resembles a gigantic golf ball. They stand in a sheltered alcove overlooking the massive inside space, filled with a wide variety of commercial amusement rides and activities.

Disney is astounded, "Wow! It really happened! My namesake became another reality." He suddenly stops when he hears a gasp from behind.

A delicate-featured black man in his early 20s protests, "What? How did you get in here? This is a restricted area for …"

"Yes, son," Disney reassures him, "I know where we are and how we got here. What about you? Why are you here?"

The young man tries to navigate the unfathomable intrusion, "I'm trying to stay cool, calm, and collected before having to appear at tonight's opening of my show, Captain EO. It's a short 3-D sci-fi film about the way we are here to change the world." He points to a very long line of people milling around, waiting to enter a theater, "It's down there."

Clemens is taken aback, "Three Dee? What in tarnation are three D's?"

Walt snickers, "Sam, 3-D is a term for three-dimensional views of objects. This type of film is a motion picture that enhances the illusion of depth perception. The most common approach to the production of 3-D films, I believe, is derived from stereoscopic photography. It was first used around 1915 and became prominent in the early 1950s. But of course you, Sam, wouldn't know about it. After all, it was after your time."

"Humph! I didn't know if Edison was up to something with his movies after I went on, or not."

"No, it was two others who worked at Edison's studio. In mid-1915, Edwin Porter and William Waddell presented tests to an audience at the Astor Theater in New York City. Because of the costly hardware and processes required to produce and display a 3 D film, it was shelved until it could be standardized decades later."

The two time travelers are standing in front of a wall photographs. The young black man looks first at Disney and Clemens, then to the photographs, and turns very pale. "What kind of a sick joke it this?"

Eepia, dressed in an elaborate, clown-like Halloween costume from an earlier encounter, speaks up, surprise and alarm evident in her voice, "Hurry, we must leave for somewhere else now! Mr. Disney your choice was not a good one this time. Choose again quickly, but be more thoughtful, please, and hurry." The crystal is glowing a deep red and releasing a strange buzzing sound.

As their bodies disappear in front of the young black man, Eepia remarks, "This is a real thriller! You both looked like your pictures on that wall you were standing in front of."

Michael Jackson tries to get a grip on what has just happened in what was supposed to be his "safe sweet suite," "Oh my, oh my, oh Lordy!" He paces, shuffles his feet back and forth, and mutters aloud, "That's an interesting idea, man in the mirror…"

∞

CHAPTER *12*

Haight–Ashbury Redux

THE San Francisco street scene is orderly, tidy, and clean. People going about their business are dressed conservatively and tastefully for winter weather. Clemens, Disney, and Eepia rematerialize swiftly, exactly where they had before. And they are amazed by the changes in the neighborhood.

Eepia sees a passerby, a woman wearing high-heeled boots and a fur-trimmed coat. Innocently, she reaches out to pet the collar. Disney grabs her hand and quickly pulls it back to save her from some embarrassment.

"Are we back in San Francisco? If so, what year is this, Eepia? I chose to see San Francisco once more to find out if it had changed any since we were there before, or to witness further moral decay."

He points to the crystal, urging her to find some answers.

Raising the crystal to her forehead, she simultaneously morphs into wearing an identical fur-collared coat. "It has been 7,304 days since our last visit and, in case you are interested, 174,296 hours, or 20 years to the day. Yes, we are in San Francisco, California. Do you need anything more?"

"No," he smiles, "I believe you have been precise enough." He murmurs to himself, She has certainly adapted to becoming precise. Yes, she is advancing in demeanor and style; she still needs more work on using language and that's Sam's particular bailiwick. He gazes around, then points to an older black man. "Look, Sam, isn't that our friend? The shopper who was so distraught?"

Clemens looks carefully and nods, his face beaming agreement. With the older gentleman is a good-looking younger version of himself and a young child, obviously a grandson.

Pride radiates from the older man as his eyes meet theirs. He nods a greeting, stops, registers confusion, then grins, knowing there can be no mistake.

He shakes his head in wonder, puts his arms around his family, and walks on down the main street. The grandfather mumbles, "Had I not been there, I wouldn't have believed it, would've said it was my imagination playing tricks on me. To those who know, no explanation is needed; to the others, none is possible." The son just looks at him, unable to fathom an answer.

The boy races ahead, holding the strings of helium-filled Mickey and Minnie balloons that fly and bump in the wind behind him. Mickey somehow gets loose and quickly floats skyward. The youngster calls out, "Look grandpa, Mickey is flying off to the moon, just like in the cartoons."

"That makes Eepia happy."

Disney matches her joy, "I know what you mean. That gentleman was so miserable when we were here last, I wondered if he would have the strength to carry on. Say, Sam, you think he recognized us?"

"Nice touch with the mouse ears on the balloon." Clemens must add his two cents. "Reminds me of myself. I was out west and was doing some mining. I got to thinking it was not worth using one more bucket of water … so I quit. The next guy who came along used that one more bucket of water and struck pay dirt exactly where yours truly once stood. The rest of my life I made myself see things through, beyond my limits if necessary. "

Disney has to ask, "How does he remind you of that?"

"When we saw that man, he was sure things would never get better. Someone more foolish might have ended it all in despair and missed the joys this man is collectin' with his family."

"That," Disney nods appreciatively. "is an important and powerful lesson for each of us. We all hit a point of despair, but it pays to be stubborn and hang around for the surprises that one more day can bring."

"Or … one more bucketful."

Eepia is warm and happy in her coat and high-heeled boots. "Why do people look different now? They changed. Eepia like them. They pretty."

"Want to field that one, Sam?"

"It seems to me that folks always do what is not expected of them. It had obviously been the norm for them to dress and act like street urchins. They reverted back to what wasn't expected of them, and fit into civilized-type living."

"I do wonder," Walt inquires, "Eepia, are we out of that Vietnam War now?"

Before she can respond and position the crystal against her forehead, a silver Mercedes 300e pulls up to the sidewalk and parks just ahead of them. A tall, clean-cut, middle- aged man gets out. He is wearing a three-piece suit and carrying a leather briefcase. He rushes past them into what was once the laundromat, now an ice cream parlor.

Eepia is excited, "That man, he's Rain."

Clemens declares, correcting her, "Weather—water from the sky—is rain. That man, Eepia, is a businessman."

She shakes her head, "Mr. Clemens no listen to Eepia. That man talk to you before. He is Rain, hippie before."

The two trade looks of disbelief and watch the door, stunned. As if in anticipation of her words, the door slowly opens. The businessman walks back out into the sidewalk and slows to look the three time travelers over. He has never seen Eepia before, but the other two …

Rain studies the two men and says, "This is unbelievable." He leans against a NO PARKING sign and sets down his briefcase.

Clemens smiles, "Excuse me, are you Rain? That long-haired, happy gay guy we met a long time ago? You sure do clean up nicely."

Rain laughs and shakes his head with disbelief. "Rain. If I had been into heavier drugs, I'd think I was having a flashback."

"What happened to you?" Disney asks, "You look wonderful. Oops, I didn't mean that as an insult!"

Rain's amusement is evident, "First of all, my name is no longer Rain. I went back to Michael, my real name, shortly after I encountered you two."

"Eepia think he pretty. Michael nice."

Clemens and Disney continue to look him over, searching for changes in the man.

"Sam, I think we have a budding teenager on our hands." Disney turns to her and gently corrects, "Men aren't pretty, Eepia. Men are handsome. Rugged."

Michael smiles, "Thank you for the compliment, young lady." He studies Disney and Clemens in turn, concluding with, "You guys are exactly the same. I mean exactly the same! Your suits are the same. Your hair is the same. Even your faces are not one bit different. How can that be? It's been close to 20 years …"

"Crystal indicates 7,304.84 days, yes, 20 years," Eepia adds.

"Exactly, huh? I can't really much doubt that. You two were instrumental in changing my life, you know."

The crystal begins flashing crimson, but the trio, fascinated, ignores it as much as possible.

Disney is touched by the startling admission and talks faster, "How? What prompted these changes specifically? Please be quick about it."

"It was the way you made your exit … and the autograph from Mark Twain."

The crystal has darkened to maroon and is emitting high-pitched intermittent beeps.

Clemens smiles, not threatened in the least. "I think that device is getting vocal to show it is sincere. It will have to exercise a little patience. I want to hear this."

"I wasn't the only one who saw your 'Star Trek'-style departure. And then I noticed the autograph and took it to an expert. He said it was valid and he didn't know how I could have gotten it transferred onto a candy wrapper."

Eepia is alarmed, the crystal is now a mean-looking dark sienna, just one shade below the maximum. "What means Star Trek?" She frowns at the pulsing crystal that's shooting angry dark red sparks. "Please hurry. Eepia not know what will happen."

Michael looks at Eepia … and slowly turns back to the men. "I don't know exactly how to put this, but she's not … one … of us. Is she?"

Clemens and Disney laugh aloud. Michael's kindness and honesty are endearing.

Disney responds, "You're the first to notice. She's very special and works hard to keep us in line. "

"There's a problem here." Clemens, winding up to pontificate, opines, "You take uncharted territory like Adam found in the Garden of Eden. He was but human—this explains it all. He did not want the apple for the apple's sake. He wanted it only because it was forbidden. That same universal law governs all of us, except for our sweet Eepia, whose sole mission it is to keep us honest."

Disney intervenes, trying is best to limit Sam's information and revelations by asking Michael questions. "Who do you think we are and precisely how did we help with these changes?"

"I don't think I really know who or what you guys are, other than time travelers maybe. If it was just an experience, a hallucination 20 years ago, it doesn't matter now. It opened an array of possibilities that changed my view of this world."

"You have to learn to edit better than this," Clemens announces. "You'd never make it as a newspaper man."

Michael is undaunted by Clemens's lack of tact, "I made a study of Samuel Clemens and used that information to make a life for myself in the yuppie commercial world. Don't know how valid it is, but I really believe Clemens would have enjoyed knowing that he is helping to urge the kids of today to exercise their creativity. Through his characters and thoughts, his words are helping today's Tom Sawyers and Huck Finns feel they are unique and worthwhile individuals. Kids whose folks looked down on them are being applauded for their talents because of a school we started in the area. Your words—or Mark Twain's words—have made a difference."

Clemens is obviously moved by what he's heard. "That humbles a person greatly."

"That's why I'm here. I stopped by to order some handmade ice cream for the party at the school. Tomorrow the kids are going to fly down to Disneyland for a celebration. Twenty of them, the go-getters as I call them, earned the money and we are taking them there for two days of absolute fun. This includes a ride on the Mark Twain Riverboat. Samuel Clemens and Walt Disney have done more for the betterment of humanity than anyone else I know."

"Eepia think she gonna cry …" Her eyes are starry with tears. She looks about helplessly for something to wipe away the tears, which are new to her.

Disney and Clemens are unable to hide the grins of joy and pride beaming on their faces.

Michael leans in close to Clemens, "Really now … who are you? Could it be a glitch in time or something? Could you really be Samuel Clemens? I know for sure you aren't Hal Holbrook. Is it really you?"

A young college-bound girl walks by and Michael points to Clemens. "Young lady, would you let your grandfather dress like this man does?"

She responds accordingly, "He has the right to dress any way he wants to, but I would think that white would be hard to keep clean." She continues on to elsewhere in somewhat of a hurry.

Michael laughs with relief, "She sees you! Thank god! I thought I might be losing my mind again. The first time wasn't so great."

The crystal is now too hot to handle. Eepia tries to hand it off to them unsuccessfully.

The trio realize they must leave right now!

Michael is taken aback by its condition, "Oh geez. Those are the same colors I saw before. You're getting ready to leave again, right?"

Clemens retorts, "Right you are son. But I must admit, this has been remarkable."

"You will never know what you have done for us, son. We're glad to know you're doing so well. You're a special person."

Disney must know, "Oh—are we out of Vietnam's war yet?"

Talking quickly Michael senses the trio ebbing away. "Yes, but it took over 10 years, and only lately has this nation barely begun to appreciate the plight of all the men and women who served in that unpopular war. We still have too many missing in action – those who never came back—more than 58,000. It's doubtful we will ever get the full truth from our government."

"Michael, you are one remarkable person." Disney is stunned, "Don't let your affluence change that."

Eepia want Michael to come with us." She is the first to dissipate into the void.

Clemens counters, "Young lady, you do not invite men … they invite you. So much to learn."

Her essence is completely dissolved, "She's your problem, Walt."

Disney is undeterred, "You've helped us to celebrate the moral indestructibility of the human species. I'm grateful for the lesson."

Michael stands unmoving as they completely disappear in a flood of sparkles, akin to a firework display. Eyes filled with tears, he waves an emotional goodbye to what is now empty space. "Even if I imagined the whole thing, I wouldn't have missed it!"

He looks down and realizes a candy bar lies at his feet, bearing the message:

Often it takes two visits to make a sale. Are you sold on the enormities of life? Mark Twain.

∞

CHAPTER *13*

It's Disco Time in a Big City

LOUD music is everywhere, blaring from multiple stacks of loud speakers spaced less than ten feet apart on every wall, even the pillars. Mirrored balls and laser lights glint and flash, bathing the raucous crowd of unrefined revelers in spangles and colors.

Several people dance, still holding their spilling drinks; someone kicks a crushed empty beer can and it clatters across the sticky dance floor, coming to rest right in front of Clemens and Disney as they appear. No one even notices their arrival. They are standing in front of a long-haired, five-member group, "Hurnia," a local hard-rock band.

They freeze in disbelief.

Eepia appears, dressed as a ballerina, her hair tightly combed into a bun, from another year's influence. Turning this way and that, soaking up the atmosphere in wonder and fear, she energetically morphs into a pastiche of the people in the room. Her hair stands up in points of red, purple, and green. A chain of entwined safety pins forms a necklace that droops down and across her mid-chest. White and black face paint all but obliterates her delicate eyes. Although she appears to be wearing leathers, they are torn and tattered and have deliberately provocative slits, creating an unbecoming style.

In mental anguish, Clemens looks around and passes judgment, "I want no part of this."

"This is a true culture shock." Disney is aghast, "I wonder what can be gained from this stopover. I don't know what I was thinking."

Eepia is intrigued by a young man across the room, near the very back. It's a little quieter there, making it possible to actually hear the person next to you. She smiles at him and he approaches her slowly, motioning for her to join him at a nearby table.

She naïvely agrees and sits beside him.

Noticing how buxom and alluring the women have made a point of being, her figure responds and fills out to more than ample proportions. This does not go unnoticed by Clemens and Disney, as well as Eepia's new admirer.

"Hi. I'm a Libra. What's your sign?"

Her mind whirls for an answer, "Mr. Clemens read it to Eepia. "No parking between the hours of 6:30 A.M. and 4:30 P.M."

The admirer laughs heartily, "I don't believe in that garbage myself. You are charming."

Eepia smiles, she seems attracted to him. He looks deeply into her eyes. Clemens and Disney are bemused by her actions. "My name is Scott. What is yours?"

"Eepia." Blushes coyly, "Eepia New Soul."

"Pretty name. Exotic. Is this your first time here?"

"First time. Yes."

Scott is intrigued, exclaiming, "You're so shy. Completely different from what your appearance projects. A real paradox."

Clemens grows concerned and wants to rescue Eepia from the grips of the admirer.

Disney holds him back. "It seems this stop might very well be for our Eepia's benefit. She is learning about exchanges with another human being. We can help her, but only if she needs it."

A middle-aged woman with an overly painted face, wearing sparkling emerald heels and a matching sequined miniskirt, dances over and nudges Clemens with her hip. In a slurred Southern accent, she asks him to join her, "Ya wanna dance hunny?"

He is dumbfounded and simply stares at her, not knowing what to do or say.

She quickly shrugs her shoulders and dances away to find another likely partner.

....

"Eepia, you obviously don't fit the Punk mold." Scott is intrigued, "Why would you make yourself look like this?"

"Eepia want to belong ... to learn who she is."

"You talk ... so hesitantly. I don't think I have a real grasp of who you are." He is sincere, "It doesn't matter, somehow. I genuinely like you. I don't understand it, but I feel protective. I guess that's the term."

She points to a voluptuous girl nearby, "Do Scott like that girl?"

He looks then, "Yeah, I guess so."

Her chest swells larger, "Do Scott like Eepia better now?"

He's astounded at the sight, "What are you doing? Are we on Candid Camera? That's it, isn't it? We're on a television show."

"Eepia not understand. Does Scott not like Eepia better now?"

Scott looks around and realizes there are no cameras—the quirky girl is for real. "Stop it! You don't need to inflate yourself to get me to like you. Geez, I'm attracted to what you are inside. One Dolly Parton in the world is wonderful; two is more than the world needs. I like you just the way you are."

Eepia smiles and her blouse size slims down to normal proportions. She grins and looks away from his gaze. "Eepia want to talk to Scott about his life. What makes you laugh and what makes you cry?"

"I laugh at—oh let's see... I laugh at the antics of new puppies playing in the sunshine. I cry when I see acts of kindness beyond normal reactions. Jokes don't make me laugh, but human foibles do. I cry when I hear music that touches me or watching reunions of people who love each other. What about you?"

She shyly responds, "This is first conversation Eepia--I--ever really have. I think I cry when someone is sad or hurt. I laugh when Mr. Clemens say things he knows will shock people. He is very funny man. Sad, too, sometimes, but funny most of the time I've known him."

Clemens is concerned because he and Disney are several tables away. "She may be too naïve to be with the likes of that man in public. You know, all I have to do is sign an autograph and we're gone in a flash. I'll deal with Gabriel soon enough."

"Uh-huh. Thought you couldn't be bothered with new souls, insisted they are a pain. Isn't that what you said?"

Clemens frowns, focuses his attention on the two. "Yes, but she is so naïve... probably telling him she is a new soul from Heaven and here trying out life. Oh my! Look! Look what's happening to her hair!"

Eepia's hair is changing colors, falling softly to her neck, brown and shiny. She looks beautiful. Her clothes are becoming very simple and modest. Scott appears not to be seeing the changes right in front of his eyes; he is enjoying the conversation, lost in the dialogue.

"Why did you come here tonight?" Eepia's conversation is getting better, as she relaxes into the newfound friendship.

"I am writing an article for a local newspaper." He is astonished by his own admission, "I can't believe I told you that. I was doing it incognito."

"But why did you choose me to talk with?"

"I don't know." He eases into speaking the simple truth, "You seemed to be a stereotype of a punk rocker, but when I looked into your eyes, there was something so pure. That sounds so trite, but it's true."

"I am glad you talked to me. I feel happy inside. More alive."

Scott is at a loss for words. Eepia smiles, exhilarated. Clemens is furious as he watches them.

Disney is conciliatory, "I think perhaps you had better deal with what is irritating you."

"That's all well and good for you to say—I don't know what has me so angry."

"I think I know. You are re-experiencing the painful feelings a father has when he sees his little girl growing up."

Clemens' eyes moisten, "And maybe not needing us near as much."

When Scott offers his hand to her she accepts. She also leaves the crystal on the table. Eepia laughs while Scott moves them onto the dance floor and teaches her a modern dance. She is radiant. Scott is completely enchanted, too.

Disney and Clemens see the crystal fire up a distinctive red glow, wondering what that signals, but decide instead to watch before acting.

"Also," Disney observes, "she has become a participant, rather than just an observer."

"Yes, you're right, Walt, She's no longer an observer of life. It's a lot like giving birth and watching the growing process in a compressed time span—and a whole lot less expensive."

Scott, feeling so much in so little time, is unnerved. "I've never felt like this before. I don't want this night to end. You don't threaten any part of my personality. You enhance what I believe in. We make an extraordinary team; don't you see it too?"

Eepia notices the angry red crystal on the small table nearby at last, and her eyes fill with tears. "Scott, I must go now. Do not be sad and do not think what we shared is or was not true. I have only a small time to spend with you and have to obey all my instructions. We will laugh again. Not here, but far away and we will remember. Now, I ask you to trust Eepia and turn away."

Scott is horrified at this speech. He holds onto her arm and looks intensely into her eyes. "Don't you dare leave me now! I just found you! If you are in some sort of trouble, let me help you. Just stay. I have connections with City Hall and on Capitol Hill. Please, I can't lose you. I don't know what is happening to me, but you can't go! I—I need you, Eepia."

She stands on her tiptoes and hugs Scott tightly. He takes her face into his hands and kisses her tenderly. Tears fill their eyes, and she turns him gently to face another direction.

She looks around to pick up the red crystal but it is no longer on the table they recently occupied. Someone must have taken it, maybe it was her mentors and confidants?

No, Clemens and Disney are alarmed because they, too, missed the snatch and grab.

....

"Sam, we gotta find that damnable thing quick!" Disney then sees it in the hands of a female employee and exclaims, "Oh my Gawd!" As she stashes it in one of her baggy pockets, she also immediately cries out in panic; the crystal changes everything.

Within seconds, the errant server levitates into midair and dematerializes within view of several of the less inebriated patrons, whose puzzled looks shift to absolute amazement

In a brilliant flashing multicolored blazing display, Disney, Clemens, and Eepia also disappear.

Scott, feeling bereft, turns around slowly to find her gone.

....

They are in freefall in a familiar golden elevator. Everyone is panicked.

Clemens is totally unnerved and barks, "What in tarnation is happening?"

Even more startling, the server, holding the crystal, appears with them.

Disney shouts, "We're in for it now. We're on the fast track going down to You-Know-Where! How are we going to stop it? Eepia, help us!"

She is terrified, "I'm trying, but I don't know how! Mr. Clemens, help us!"

"Been down this road before; 'taint no picnic; even wrote about it once or twice."

Disney sees a red panic button on the elevator wall and smashes his hand against it.

No response.

"So much for your confounded rhetoric and no action!"

Clemens mumbles, "Oh how about giving this old man a break will you?"

The female employee's fear is out of control. "Holy shit!" she screams, "What is happening, where is this, why are we going down, and where?"

Disney is both intrigued and concerned, "In which order do you want the answers?"

Clemens reacts, "I don't believe she cares one way or the other; just get on with it!"

"OK then, let me inquire…" and loudly calls, "oh Gabriel?"

Gabriel's alarmed voice reverberates in the small falling compartment, "I told you this might happen. Now what do you expect me to do about it, fix it in spite of everything?"

They enthusiastically nod their heads, not able to speak.

The server who initiated this conversation is close to total hysteria.

Gabriel avers, "No can do. Your collective beds have been made, now you all get to experience the next stage, unless..."

Disney grasps at any straw offered to him, "Unless what, please hurry!"

Clemens reacts differently, "I'm gettin' a nosebleed! Eepia, hand me a hankie!"

Eepia retorts "I don't know what a hankie is! Help!"

Gabriel makes himself heard above the trivialities, "...unless I can get some divine intervention, next stop is at the bottom of it all, and I guarantee you won't like it one little bit!"

The poor server who has joined them unwittingly cries out, "In the name of all that's everywhere present, all powerful, all knowing, intervention is paramount! If what I did is unforgivable, don't let the others suffer for my mistake! I did not know what this glowing orb was. I thought it might be a nice addition to my rock collection. Here, take it back!" She tosses it in the air, trusting someone will catch it.

Eepia does and the elevator slows to a halt. "Oh thank God!" they sigh in unison.

Gabriel seems pleased with their thinking and responses. "Anything else any of you care to share at this time? This elevator is very close to ground zero, if you know what I mean."

The walls seem to be heating up.

Disney, thinking lightning quick , suggests, "What about a divine re-set, is that possible?"

"Unlikely, but... yes, it's possible, if..." absolute stillness prevails. They hold their breath until he speaks again. "It may be possible to use the Law of Unintended Consequences."

Clemens cries out in anguished liberation, "Now that's a law I can deal with; it seems I may have broken one or two of the others lately."

Disney is even quicker to admonish his mentor, "Yes Sam, I can safely admit it, you have been a mite reckless so far in my adventure. "

Gabriel's tone changes, "Be careful Walt, remember the adage about those who live in glass houses ought not to throw stones."

"OK, OK, I admit it, maybe I did pull a prank or two on Sam while we were cruising about the timelines. You do know my history as a practical joker, right"

Gabriel responds accordingly, "Right. A snake is just a snake until it lets loose its venom. Eepia, what about you? It's your turn."

"I became a trifle engaged in dancing with Scott and left the crystal on the table for anyone to pick it up. I am so very sorry for my indiscretion and lack of attention to my duty."

"OK then, that's much better Eepia. And you, Kathryn Sullivan, you are accountable as well."

Kathryn is astounded, "How... do... you know... my name? I was just a passerby cleaning up after the partygoers and noticed this glowing object on the table and I thought maybe some of the customers had left already, so I was doing what I was supposed to do, honest."

"And," Gabriel inquires, "where were you going with it? To put the glowing orb in the lost and found maybe?"

Kathryn is definitely embarrassed, "Oops, I see what you are getting at."

Gabriel changes the subject, "Kathryn, are you or are you not in the NASA astronaut's program?"

Her mouth drops open in absolute amazement, "Yes. I was on a leave of sorts and was helping out a friend while she was incapacitated for a few days. How do you know?"

Disney is tickled, "You're an astronaut? Have you been in space yet?"

Clemens proudly baits her, "Or to the moon yet? We have."

Kathryn looks at them carefully, "I remember hearing rumors flying about it after I joined the Corps. Are you telling me the three of you were there? How? Why? Oh wow, I feel faint...."

She collapses and slumps to the floor, out like a light.

"Sam, now you've really exceeded your quota of missteps." Disney looks up, "What do we do now Gabriel?"

"Samuel Langhorne Clemens, this time you have actually helped instead of hindered. As a result, you've just earned your first merit. Walt, look at the top left corner if you care to." He does, and a smile crosses his face and smooths his crinkled brow.

"Yes, way up there. See the little button the size of a pea? Press it, and I don't care how you do it, but do it soon. The temperature is getting hotter by the moment where you are now and if you wait much longer, well, it'll be time for a bar-be-cue of an unpleasant sort, get my drift?"

Disney immediately looks around and up, focusing on the button, "Eepia, climb on my shoulders and hurry!"

She struggles at first trying to get on his shoulders, Clemens offers and helps by giving her a boost up. She stretches as high as she can but it's not enough. "Mr. Clemens, please hand me the crystal and don't you dare drop it!"

Clemens does exactly as she asks. Eepia has to toss the crystal three times, targeting its trajectory at the tiny little star-shaped button; she connects just in time. The walls are steaming hot.

Suddenly, someone or something outside is pounding heavily on the elevator door. The elevator shudders as it starts, then slowly ascends and the air progressively cools as they rise up, and up, and up.

Not knowing where they are going to land, they are just happy to be moving upward, gaining altitude and speed ... and then, the elevator stops and the doors slide open. They are back at the disco; it's empty. Kathryn Sullivan is still unconscious, sprawled on the elevator floor.

Disney sweating and Clemens grunting, they carry her to a booth and leave her there to awaken by herself. They quickly return to the elevator.

Eepia cautiously inquires, "Please excuse me for asking this Gabriel, but what happens to Scott?" She checks to see if the crystal might answer. It doesn't.

"Eepia, Orson Scott Card is now scheduled to become a famous author, writing science fiction stories, stemming from the experience he thought he had here. And Kathryn Sullivan will not only be the first woman to walk in space, she might also become the head of NOAA."

Clemens is amused and suggests, "You mean to tell me she is gonna build an ark too?"

It's Disney's turn to answer, "No Sam, N-O-A-A was the first scientific agency, long before even you were a gleam in your parents' eyes, or thought of. Gabe, is this the time? Do we come back with you now or not?"

"Walt, do you think you are adequately prepared and ready to make an informed decision?"

"No, not yet. I hope I still have a few stops left to gather as much as I can before I decide ... one way or the other. We're still in the eighties, right?"

"OK then," Gabriel explains, "The Law of Unintended Consequences has been sufficiently fulfilled. On this particular venture, the three of you landed in a bucket of manure and have emerged smelling like a rose. As the British say, keep calm and carry on."

Clemens laughs, "Now those were some catchy phrases! ... shoulda thought 'em up myself."

"Which one, keeping calm or the rose?" Disney addresses Gabriel, "You seemed to enjoy being boring, but after all this time you actually surprise me with your gay wit."

"Well, I'll be, you're gay too?" Clemens slaps his thigh in merriment, "Who woulda thunk?"

"Excuse me gentlemen," Eepia asks, "would either of you please explain what you both mean? Remember, I'm new and still needing to learn much."

The sparkles start to swirl around them and Walt's and Sam's chuckles become uproarious laughter. Eepia suspects she is missing out on something and frowns. The three quickly dissolve into the next thought Disney has about where to land.

CHAPTER *14*

Not a Good Day for Stocks

A KING-SIZE bed dominates the middle of the room between two large hanging ferns. The spread has soft shades of dusty rose and silver grays, and the stained glass headboard is a riot of purple grapes and bright green leaves twined through the bottom edge of a mirror. Clemens and Eepia arrive right next to the bed.

Walt materializes dangerously close to a waterfall fountain in the corner. "Oops! Seems my logistics are cutting things a bit too close."

The three delightedly set about looking into every nook and cranny to adjust to their new surroundings. Disney asks, "What year is this, Eepia? I already know this is not my Tomorrowland."

"The crystal says it is October 19, 1987, New York City. The suite we are in is leased to a Debbie Knight, a stockbroker on Wall Street."

Clemens is wearily looking around the room, "1987, eh? It has now been 77 long years since I have done a lick of exercise… I just finished an Olympic run, weathered a blaringly loud cacophony, and survived an elevator ride toward hell—o!" His attention is riveted, "That bed looks delicious."

"Mr. Clemens, doesn't delicious mean something to eat that tastes good?"

Sam takes off his shoes as he explains, "In this case it means something delightful. I think I miss that wonderful feeling a person gets just before they drop off to sleep. That safe, comfortable moment you enjoy when you have worked hard and are exhausted. You know, delicious."

"Sam," Disney cautions, "you aren't seriously going to lie down on the job now, are you?"

"I most certainly am. You youngsters go on and play; I believe I have earned a reward: a nap. After all," he beams with pride, "I've gotten my first merit."

"Yes, you did, old man," Disney is conciliatory, "and let's hope and pray it doesn't take another 77 years before you earn another one."

Clemens silently dismisses the comment and readies himself to literally dive onto the inviting bed, not in the least worried about what might happen next.

Eepia gazes at the bed without reaction other than curiosity, and she touches a button on the headboard as Clemens simultaneously lands on the bed—and immediately screams, "Oh my …!" along with a stream of expletives that fly fast and furiously from his irreverent mouth.

Large waves toss him back and forth on the bed, and Sam's face turns a shade of light green. The harder he works to get off the bed, the higher the waves become.

Disney and Eepia laugh hysterically while they attempt to pull him off the bed.

In this middle of this bedlam, the phone rings, which startles all of them. A female voice emanates from a white box inset on a shelf in the headboard, saying:

"Hi. This is Debbie. Thank you for calling. I'm in Hawaii for two glorious weeks. If you really need to get an urgent message to me, call my sister at 299-555-5555. If you would rather leave a message instead, then wait for the sound of the beep. I'll call you back, soon after I return. Aloha and Mahalo."

Beep!

"This is Joey, Deb. I hope you are having one heck of a time. We'll have dinner and you can recap your adventures when you get home."

Click!

Eepia returns her attention to Sam and the bed, presses the same headboard button again, and the sloshing waves subside. Disney releases Clemens' arms to investigate the answering device. He grins and exclaims, "These are in homes now. How wonderful!"

Sam slowly gets his equilibrium back, "What pray tell in tarnation did I step into? And what was that sound?"

"That was Debbie." Eepia responds, "She is not in now."

Disney is intrigued, "It must be some kind of a recording device triggered by the telephone call. What a marvelous way to avoid missing calls. Science is growing by leaps and bounds!"

Clemens asks, befuddled, "You want to take a guess at what happened to this bed?"

"If you work your body to the edge, Sam, you should be able to catapult yourself out by using your own leverage… unless you're too old, lame, and need more of our help." Disney is tickled pink, "It's like an air mattress, but it's filled with liquid, maybe water?"

"Humph!" Clemens growls, "I've spent many a day on water, but never experienced such a troublesome time. I must admit, though, this bed is comfortable. I'd never wholly trust it, however." He scoots to the side, pushes down on the padded frame and propels himself up and off the waterbed.

Eepia's attention, meanwhile, has been drawn elsewhere. She sticks her head around the doorway to the living room and slowly walks through it in wonder. The furnishings take her breath away. She gingerly walks through the living area to a greenhouse patio beyond it, turns, and calls to them, "I have never seen such a pretty place this side of Heaven. Would either of you like to live here? I certainly would."

Disney is intrigued by the suite's beauty and grace, and he is also struck by a new awareness. He comments to Clemens, "You know what, Sam? Our Eepia is now a conversant woman, in charge of her own identity."

He observes to Eepia, "It has been a long time since you had to be like someone else. You've learned an important truth. You never want to be an exact duplicate of someone else. Not even twins can live under that sort of social pressure. You have to feed the conscience of Eepia, nobody else's."

He glances over at the walnut-grained bookshelf, laughs, and beckons to Clemens, "Come look! Want to know what made the writer Samuel Clemens tick? It's all right here in this book." He takes down a thick book—one of many—from the neatly alphabetized shelf.

Clemens is dismissive; he's irked. "Biographies are but the clothes and buttons of the man—the biography of the man himself cannot be written."

Disney responds to the cue and quietly replaces it unopened on the shelf.

He spots a new device next to the television. The instruction manual sits on top, and he leafs through it.

Clemens studies the titles of other authors' books on the shelf besides his own works. Many of them are about analyzing the stock market, negotiating deals, and time management, and a few are by New Age heroes: Buckminster Fuller, Carl Sagan, Wayne Dyer, Erma Bombeck, Andy Rooney, Dr. Seuss, and even Robert Schuller.

Disney looks up from the manual and smiles as Eepia, who has moved back into the room from the greenhouse, steps behind the bar separating the living room from the kitchen. "What are the things in this room? I want to look at them."

Clemens continues perusing, reverently touching several volumes of books. "This lady is certainly interested in her health." He thumbs through *Fit for Life* by H. and M. Diamond, *The Rotation Diet* by Martin Katahn, and Richard Simmons' *Never-Say-Diet Book*. "Look at the medical books!" He sighs at the titles alone, *The 8-Week Cholesterol Cure* by R.E. Kowalski, Dr. Berger's *Immune Power Diet*, and Dr. Bernie Siegel's *Love, Medicine and Miracles*. "I made a point of never reading health books. If yer not careful, a person could die from a misprint." He soon wanders away; his eyes draw him to the greenhouse patio.

Disney chuckles, thoroughly enjoying himself. "Great view, isn't it?"

"I was thinking about some of the joys of the season in New England. Spring is magical. The winter snows. I do miss those experiences."

"As a kid," Walt admits, "I marveled at that experience myself. Snow could take the ugliest scenery and overnight turn it into a fantasy world."

"The most impish, active memory I have of it," Clemens readily adds, "is when we boys would try to write our names in the snow. Bear in mind, I was known as Samuel Langhorne Clemens in those days."

"And?" Disney is only half-listening as he gazes out over the Manhattan landscape.

"I never finished my name, not even once. Now, had I been Mark Twain, I would have with utmost certainty been undefeated."

"You never cease to shock me and make me laugh." Disney re-enters from the patio, "You certainly have and assuredly deserve your reputation."

"My reputation? Why, what do you — "

Eepia flips a light switch in the kitchen, but a growling sound fills the room. "Oh my goodness, HELP!"

Disney rushes to the rescue and turns it off. "It's just an ordinary garbage disposal, honey."

"A what?" She is unsettled, tense, and afraid, "I'm scared of this animal."

Disney scans the room and sees an apple on the wet bar. He takes it, turns on the water in the sink and tosses the apple into the disposal, which instantly shreds it.

Eepia and Clemens both shudder.

He then demonstrates the can opener, blender, and reads the instructions on the microwave oven door. The trash compactor and food processor make both Clemens and Eepia even less comfortable.

Nevertheless curious, Clemens is a bit more adventurous and pushes on a silver bar inside an aperture in the refrigerator door, and small ice chunks fall. He pushes it again; they cluster on a grate at the bottom of the niche.

Eepia wonders aloud about the toaster oven, electric frying pan, dishwasher, and the rest of the many gadgets and utensils on the modern kitchen counter.

"Walt, it was much simpler to have a meal in my day," Clemens says. "It seems to me all of these devices would demand the mind of Thomas Edison's offspring to dominate them. Too cantankerous, and not my cup of tea to spend any time with."

As Sam leaves the kitchenette, he sees Eepia on her knees in front of the refrigerator, trying to get a better look up into the ice maker.

"Come look at this Sam." Walt has returned to the living room and is nearly beside himself with glee, "It's called a V-C-R. It has a camera on it and, if I am reading this right, it will take photographs and play them right back. And this is for home use? Simply amazing!"

Clemens could not care less, "I saw a moving picture about a landing on the moon way back in the day; never thought it was more than a mindless episode in someone's imagination. My friend Tom Edison took a picture, a kinescope I think he called it, of me walking, but that was some years later."

"I believe you Sam, I remember seeing that a long, long time ago. Look how far we have come." He turns on the large bulky color television. The first station is showing a rerun of "Bonanza."

It takes Clemens' breath away. He sits down on a large white hassock, entranced. "Say there ... isn't that near where we were when I saw the younger version of myself?"

Instead of answering, Disney switches channels with the remote control as he sits on the sofa. The movie, "It Happened One Night" plays in black and white as Clark Gable—in a most memorable scene, especially for the year it was made—removes his shirt and reveals his bare chest.

"Now that is more like the days I knew," Clemens exclaims, "Better, but still black and white and grays."

Eepia looks at the movie, "How was it to live in the days without color? I think it would be sad ... and ... blah." She takes a moment to stare, "I think I have seen a picture of that man in Gabriel's office."

Disney chuckles, "The days were not black and white, honey. The pictures were photographed that way. Our real life was filled with color just like now. And yes, there is an autographed picture of Mr. Gable in Gabriel's office."

Eepia decides to perch on the sofa and enjoy the entertainment too. "I am so glad. I felt sorry for you Mr. Sam, colorless."

Clemens resumes his normal witty observations, "See ... that's what I mean about new souls. Just when you think they understand they go and make unsatisfactory remarks like that."

Disney changes the channel again. "Look!" Delighted, he puts down the remote while the screen shifts from character to character to identify the channel. "They call this station the DISNEY CHANNEL! There's my Mickey Mouse character. And his nemesis Donald Duck, and Tom Sawyer and Huck Finn. I am simply amazed!"

Clemens picks up the remote and pushes a button. Instantly they see a scene from Blue Hawaii with Elvis Presley singing "The Wedding Song." He watches silently, stunned.

Disney enthusiastically picks up the video camera next to the television and presses the red Record button. It lights up red.

Suddenly Eepia's crystal begins to flash an alarming, angry crimson.

Disney points the camera at Clemens, who protests, "Are you taking pictures with that contraption?"

"Yes ... I think I am."

"You know what some Indian folks believed about photographs? They felt you imprisoned a part of a person's soul and, well, I have little enough to go around."

Eepia looks concerned then confused, "Mr. Clemens isn't doing anything bad, yet the crystal is blaringly mad. What is wrong?"

"This is extraordinary!" Clemens is deliriously excited, "I hope the respected hierarchy in Heaven is taking notes. Walter is the culprit. This is exhilarating to actually be blame-free!"

Disney is focused solely on the camera. "I bet it is because I am using this camera. I just need to see if it will play back."

Flashing a deep, dark red, the crystal is now continuously blaring a staccato Beep! Beep! Beep! that gains in volume until it reaches near eardrum-shattering decibel levels.

Disney pays it no heed; he quickly searches the instruction manual and follows the directions. With uncanny precision and intense focus born of his years in the editing room, he rewinds to the number he started with on the digital connection, attaches the camera cable to the back of the television, then pushes the button marked PLAY.

A snowy image at first, then they see a sharp, clear picture of Sam Clemens talking moments before. "That is unnerving. I never thought I looked or sounded like that," Clemens says. He points, "Look, Eepia, that's you!"

Eepia is intrigued and leaves the crystal behind while she approaches the TV screen. "How did you do that? How can Mr. Clemens and I be there and here at the same moment? How did we get in there?"

Clemens points to Eepia, "For once, I am with her. How did you do it?"

A rainbow-sparkling field shimmers suddenly around all three and they quickly scamper to gather around the crystal.

Disney looks back in panic at the camera and TV, realizing he has not erased the tape and, although he turned off the TV, Samuel Clemens and Eepia will be the first thing the owner of the apartment will see when she turns on the set.

Clemens can't keep himself from laughing, "It is great to be guilt free. I am ashamed of you, Walt. Yessiree, I thought you were of higher moral fiber..."

The phone rings and rings; the answering mechanism activates, beeps. "Holy hell-o Debbie! Call me ASAP, shit! What's that sister's number again?

The stock markets in Hong Kong and Europe have crashed and now it's the U.S.! It looks like you may be a much broker broker after all this is over."

As they dematerialize in the sparkling cloud Disney asks, "I wonder what that phone message was all about."

∞

CHAPTER *15*

Tiananmen Square, China

WHEN they reappear, Disney and Clemens are dumbfounded as they watch, fascinated by a young college-aged man standing alone, dressed simply in a white shirt and black trousers in front of a column of green camouflage-painted tanks, each with a red five-pointed star on its turret; dust fiercely whips and swirls around him. Is it for protection from the onslaught of the advancing menace? Are these metal warriors on wheels?

As the tank moves to circumvent him, he moves to stay directly in its path, dangerously so. Many others watch helplessly from the filthy streets, littered not just with trash but with bodies no longer among the living. The atmosphere is hostile.

Disney is immediately affronted by a rotten odor and, alarmed, asks, "Eepia, if it's not too much trouble, would you please tell me what we're watching, where we are, why I am here, why the streets are so littered with trash, and what's that gawdawful smell?"

She has fixated instead on something more immediate: a flower in all its brilliance is growing up from a small crack at the edge of the vast expanse of concrete in the square. It has vibrant yellow petals and a black center. "Oh, such a pretty thing in all this hardness." She is undeterred by the scene unfolding at the northern edge of the square and marvels only at this single flower standing tall, almost as if it were as defiant as the lone, slender man holding his ground not too far from her.

"Eepia, did you not hear Walt ask you a question?" Clemens turns to Disney, "Walt, it looks like we may be on our own for this one. She seems to be transfixed on that lonely little flower."

Only when she registers hearing nearby mechanical rumblings does she respond. "That pretty little flower, is it going to be OK?"

The lead tank tries again to maneuver by the unknown man; he carries two shopping bags and shifts his position repeatedly to obstruct the tank's path around him.

Cameras are catching it live and broadcasting the scene around the world.

"Eepia is concerned, are those machines going to run over him too? Why is he in such a dangerous spot?"

Clemens exclaims, "That man is a dunderhead!"

The crystal is glowing and pulsating before Eepia realizes it. "Crystal already beeping and we just arrived here. Why?"

Disney is in a quandary and asks tersely, "That's what I've wanted you to tell me, if it's not too much trouble."

"Oh, is that what you were asking? I'm sorry Mr. Disney, it's just that the little flower is all alone and in harm's way, and maybe that man in front of those big angry-looking machines is too. Is that what you wanted to know?"

Walt really doesn't know how to reply. "What am I supposed to think about this? Could it be something about China's First Emperor, Qin, and his terracotta army in a tomb that was unearthed?"

Gabriel's voice answers him. "Maybe, and maybe more than you can imagine. Catch it on the 11 o'clock news. You'll figure it out soon enough. Time's a-wasting. You must leave now!"

"But Gabe," Disney resists, "we just got here, wherever this here is! Who is that youngster and what year is this, too? I'm totally confused. We've been here only a few minutes, if that."

"No time for questions. That young man you are watching has deliberately placed himself in danger; the irony is the street name: The Avenue of Eternal Peace. Nothing here you need to see any more of. Get Sam and Eepia back here pronto. This stopover was not on the roster of serious possibilities. It's completely out of our hands."

"You mean it's a wild card of sorts?" Clemens has avoided seeing what may be unfolding by looking at the trees alongside the wide avenue. Thinking aloud, he comments, "Wild card … I was a bit of one in my youth, weren't you Walt? I know my stuff when it comes to card games; had enough of it when I was tramp steaming so long ago down the Mississippi."

"What's a wild card?" Eepia doesn't understand, "I would like to know, please."

"Not now Eepia," Gabriel insists, "maybe later."

Before our travelers totally dissolve from sight and this experience, they see the young man let fly an oddly shaped helium balloon he had stashed in one of the shopping bags; he is hustled away by several Chinese military.

It's Mickey Mouse, with ears.

It launches upward into the cloudy skies and Disney feels humbled. "Seems as if my mouse idea has spread far and wide, more than I ever thought possible. I have long wondered what the marketing department has been up to. Now I have a hint of a glimmer…"

"Walt, where do you think we're going this time?"

"To be honest Sam, I don't have a clue; this is far more than Mr. Toad's Wild Ride." Disney is deeply concerned, "Could it be something more horrible than I might need to bear witness to, or be involved in to even the minutest extent? This one has taken me by surprise. Only God must know."

CHAPTER 16

Berlin's Falling

THOUSANDS of people are amassed, watching and waiting, gathered in front of a huge wall that has blocked half the city from the other for more than 20 years. It's Berlin, Germany, on November 9, 1989.

Jubilant revelers have hammers and are pounding on the massive, colorful, and graffiti-covered wall. Eepia doesn't understand, "The artwork is so pretty! Why are so many trying to hurt it?"

Disney smiles and gently explains, "Our naive Eepia—years ago, in 1961, they built this wall and divided a city in two. It seemed to come up almost overnight."

Clemens' response is not as warm-hearted. "Well, I'll be hornswoggled. Someone musta been very, very mad to do this sort of thing. Who in their right mind would do this anyway?"

"Sam, this is not the time for a history lesson in world politics, as much as you'd most likely be entertaining." Disney is conciliatory. "For now, let's just find out what is going on. I can only hope this is not like what we nearly witnessed in China. From what Eepia divined from the crystal, we got out of there in the nick of time."

"Yes, almost by the skin of my incisors," Clemens says, thinking he is being clever, "if I may make so bold a reference."

"Is that an idiom or a hyperbole Mr. Clemens?" Eepia asks sweetly. "I have been learning much in a very short time. If I understand correctly, teeth have no skin and it is not to be taken literally."

"Yes, Eepia dear," Disney agrees, "your vocabulary and articulation are profoundly improved of late."

Jumping back in to change the subject, Clemens declares, "Speakin' of politics. As I recall, poly means many and ticks are blood suckin' insects. Do we still have that blight in Washington, D.C.?"

Disney chuckles at the metaphor. "I suppose they still do."

Clemens looks more closely at the wall then comments, imagining, "Iffen you have a hankering to, I could round up some whitewash and go to town on this wall. Kinda reminds me of a story I wrote, Tom Sawyer. Eepia could play Becky Thatcher and you could be my friend Huck Finn … whaddya think?"

"I am to be Becky Thatcher? Who is she? I like me now. Why would I wish to change into someone I'm not? Please explain."

Clemens begins but is interrupted by Disney. "Fear not, dear, he is not asking you to change. Mr. Clemens was suggesting we recreate an episode from a much-loved and often-read story he wrote about early childhood life on the Mississippi River. As I recall, that particular book was banned from many libraries."

A shocked look on his face, Clemens snickers, "Seems like some of my works grated strongly on the nerves of a few silly thinkin', bubble-headed, narrow-minded persons of literary say-so; they also expressed very little integrity other than their own simple-minded biases. Those same critics never wrote a lick of their own words either and published them, unless it was to inflame the public and puff up their own egos. Boston never has been one of my favorite places to visit. But when my works in Boston were banned it promoted my distribution instead; it had the opposite effect on book buyers."

Disney can't help himself and interjects, "During that period, Boston officials had the authority to ban works featuring 'objectionable' content and often banned works containing sex or foul language."

Sam's face contorts, "I take umbrage at that! There weren't nuthin' sexual about my words. I simply objected to their banning how I used colorful language of the times, that's all."

Eepia points to water rushing through the wall, "Look, a waterfall through a wall … how can that can be?"

Disney tries to explain, "The water is from a fire hose on the other side, Eepia. In this case it looks like East is going to meet West with the help of all these people. Overnight on August 13, 1961, this imposing physical concrete barricade divided eastern from western Berlin. The Soviets wanted to prevent mass emigrations to the West.

"Then-President Kennedy spoke two memorable phrases in a 1963 speech that said volumes to West Germany, Ich bin ein Berliner, 'I am a Berliner,' and Lass' Sie nach Berlin kommen, 'let them come to Berlin' addressing the Communists. The Berlin Wall became the most enduring symbol of the Cold War."

"Cold War … I've never heard of such a thing." Clemens questions, "To me all wars were bloody. How was this any different?"

"George Orwell coined the term Cold War after the first atomic bombs were dropped in 1945. It described a world in which the two major powers—each possessing nuclear weapons and thereby threatening mutually assured destruction—could do so with no direct military combat."

"My experience with the un-Civil War in the 1860s is my only recollection of armed conflict." Clemens shudders, "This is so much more horrifyin', the likes of which I do not wish anyone ever to bear. Glad we missed that China uprising. That coulda been detrimental to my soul's growth. I guess I was mistaken after all."

"Hold on to that thought, Sam. I sense something wonderful is about to happen. Let's just watch for a bit, OK?"

Clemens mumbles unintelligibly.

Eepia is fascinated and, trying to take it all in, experiences a stream of icy cold water that soaks her to the skin. The crystal orb begins to glow red and pulses the longer she stays in the streaming waterworks.

Until now, her figure has been well covered. With each clothes change during or after visiting a previous time, Eepia has been an increasingly attractive female; sometimes somewhat brazen, sometimes innocent. Her waterlogged Chinese embroidered silk blouse reveals the woman's body under it right through the material, alarming both men. She doesn't know a thing about brassieres.

Clemens yells above the noisy crowd, "Walt, you are far more physically agile than I. I sense her need to be removed from this atmosphere as it could be detrimental to the goings-on, especially with those foggy-eyed ragamuffins looking her way with not-so-nice thoughts."

The crystal continues to signal timeline interference is imminent.

Disney rushes to Eepia, grabs her arm and pulls her away from the spray.

"Oooh, that was so cold!" She wraps her arms around herself, then opens them again to Walt's dismayed embarrassment. "It does things to my body," she says with total innocence, "look."

He glances around, swiftly grabs a coat abandoned nearby and covers her up.

The crystal's warnings subside to a neutral, benign glow.

"What in tarnation, li'l lady," Clemens is alarmed, "were you thinkin'?"

"I'm sorry, did I offend the crystal?" Eepia wonders sheepishly, "That was not my purpose. I only wanted to feel what water was like."

"Looks to me you found out quickly enough," Clemens retorts, "And then some." "There are other ways to experience water, most of which should be conducted in a bathroom sink, or bath… and not in public as a misbehavin' spectacle."

"I have so much to learn. I'll try to be more careful." She is grateful for the coat Walt has found for her and pulls it tightly around her. She shivers.

Disney picks up a newspaper on the ground and sees the day's date: November 11, 1989. Although the words are in German, the date is unmistakable. "Looks like this date is as significant as when armistice was declared at the end of the First World War. That was supposed to be the war to end all wars. It wasn't, of course. At least this event has a better meaning for Europe."

"Hold on," declares Eepia, "the crystal indicates it is time for us to go elsewhere. This has been such a refreshing experience. Is this like one of your E-ticket rides, Mr. Disney?"

He laughs at the association. The three clasp hands and, as they fade from view, a BBC photographer pans across the scene to capture images to broadcast during the evening news. He scans the crowd to catch the history-making Berlin Wall spectacle in action and includes the three travelers' transition.

....

The British photojournalist, later ensconced in his makeshift darkroom, is astonished by what he captured. His panoramic shot of the symbolic event also recorded three figures surrounded by a colorful rainbow aura as they dissolved into nothingness.

He deletes the segment from the clip submitted to nightly world news broadcasts, but not from his personal archive.

∞

CHAPTER *17*

Mr. Toad's Wild Ride

WHEN the three rematerialize, they are instantly mesmerized by their spacious surroundings and panoramic view and try to guess where and when they are. A large metropolitan city spreads out below them in all directions.

Towering skyscrapers are everywhere. Disney is taken aback by the sights far and wide, awed by it all. He looks down at what once was touted as the world's tallest building, the Empire State building, and realizes they are standing in both an observatory and food court somewhere high up in a very crowded New York City.

Behind one of the counters a large wall clock indicates the hour with 12 hot dogs in buns. A neon sign blinks, NOW CLOSED, OPEN AT 11.

Disney fishes for money in his pockets, "Look, Nathan's hot dogs! I'm hungry." He eagerly moves toward an empty counter and no staff in sight. Eepia and Clemens remain intrigued by the incredible, breathtaking view, not caring about food. "Drats, I was so looking forward to something tasty."

Disney realizes they are the only ones in the whole area. "Eepia, what's up with this trip? I realize where we are now, but when and how high up?"

Sam is feeling his usual sarcastic self, "I'd say we're somewhere near nose-bleed city."

"Sadly no, Mr. Clemens, you are incorrect." Eepia is curious too. "The crystal indicates we are on the 107th floor of a skyscraper tower in the Manhattan area of New York City about 1,100 feet up. The date is September 11, 2001, the time is 8:38 a.m. to be precise."

She is suddenly alarmed when the crystal abruptly, violently pulses purple. "We must leave from here, now!" Her arms flail involuntarily, gesturing toward something skyward and moving. "What is this? Look at what's coming our way!"

Clemens doesn't want to shift away so soon after being at the Berlin Wall. The sudden materializing and dematerializing have left him feeling a bit nauseated. The transitions are playing games with his nervous system. He protests, "We just arrived and I want to experience the grandeur of it all."

119

But he looks where Eepia is pointing and demands, "What in tarnation is that? Bigger than anything I've ever seen, and it looks like it's definitely coming our way. Oh good Lord!"

Disney exclaims, "Holy sh--!" He yells as loud and urgently as he can, "Gabriel, get us out of here right now!"

A 767 Boeing airliner is on a direct path toward imminent collision and seems to be headed for the building right where the trio is standing. They are petrified and helpless to do anything but watch in horror. They are so close, they even see men in the cockpit staring at them.

All too quickly the nose of the jumbo jet smashes into the building's windows—just as our heroes dissolve.

Disney is extremely shaken, "What in the world was that all about? This is the second time we've been placed in harm's way. Is this what the world's coming to?"

No answer is forthcoming.

. . . .

The next instant they are on a bright sunny beach, watching with thousands of people looking at the sky, and all of them are pointing upward.

They watch as it unfolds. People of all shapes and sizes wearing sunglasses are witnessing history. A large ball of flame is propelling a shiny cylindrical object, a rocket vehicle, and it violently explodes far up in the clear blue atmosphere. The crowd's excited cheering quickly becomes astonished cries of anguish.

Disney is deeply alarmed at the violence he has seen and encountered, "Jesus H. Kee rist, Eepia, what's this?"

She looks grief-stricken as she positions the crystal at her forehead. "The crystal indicates February 1, 2003. We are witnessing a second space program accident that killed all seven crew members. As a result, all further missions into space will be curtailed for several years. The first occurrence was Space Shuttle Challenger disaster that occurred on January 28, 1986, when NASA's Space Shuttle orbiter Challenger broke apart 73 seconds into its flight, which led to the deaths of its seven crew members, too. The spacecraft we are witnessing now disintegrates over the Atlantic Ocean, off the coast of Cape Canaveral, Florida. This incident effectively grounds the entire shuttle fleet while scientists dedicate themselves to improving many safety measures and a better solid rocket booster design, and before management makes decisions about any future launches into space. Need I elucidate more?"

"Eepia, your grasp of words and speech has definitely improved since we first began this journey; I'm impressed."

"Thank you, Mr. Disney, but all I was doing is reading what has been reported. These are not my words."

"Regardless, your patterning is quite remarkable, and so sad you are having to report this type of factual information. It's making me feel as if our entire planet is not happy. Is she beginning to run amuck in response to all of industries' mechanizations and resultant pollutants, possibly?"

Irritation registering clearly on his face, Clemens remarks, "She seems almost a bit too persnickety if you ask me. Humph."

"Sam, are you affronted by Eepia's grasp of the language, or are you referring to a disaster impacting our planet?" Disney is trying his best to remain unaffected. "Whichever 'she' you mean, get your own bloated nothingness out of the way. Eepia is still new to all this, while you were around for two cycles of Haley's comet and then another 97 years of puttering around the clouds, give or take. And our planet has been around for much longer."

Clemens sulks, deciding to be silent for the time being.

"Eepia, dare I ask," Disney audibly sighs, "are there any other catastrophes I should be aware of or at least apprised about?"

She answers his question with other questions, "Do you wish to view, be involved, or be witness to more of what has actually happened during the last fifty earth cycles?"

Disney stops in his tracks to consider and elects to change the subject. "Sam, do you know the story about being involved or committed?"

"No, since I have usually been the one to wring a yarn or three, go ahead," from under his breath, "if you think you can do any better."

"I, Eepia, would like to know too."

"Well, OK then. There was a farmer and of course he had a farm with all sorts of livestock, specifically chickens and pigs. One day he decided to eat some ham and eggs for breakfast." He stopped before going any further. It didn't take long at all.

"What's so important," quips Clemens, "about wanting to have that kind of breakfast anyway?"

"I'm getting to it. You see, when the chicken laid an egg, only the hen was involved, but the pig had to be committed to provide the necessary sustenance for the farmer and his family."

"So what or how does that relate to what Eepia just articulated?"

"When we are on the ground looking at a rocket going up in space, we are only involved as witnesses, but if we were onboard, then we'd be committed."

"What about the folks who worked on the rockets; how do you think they feel when the sky lights up with what we just saw?"

An older, bald-headed man with long sideburns, dressed in an Epcot Center T-shirt and Bermuda shorts, stands near them. He is extremely upset. He turns on them and insists, "What are you yapping about? Can't you see what a disaster this is?"

"Yes, I can identify with it, of course," Disney responds. "Please excuse us. If I seem indifferent, that is not why we are here." He turns to Eepia still holding the crystal, and quietly says, "Eepia, I think we've seen enough here, let's go elsewhere. I think this roller coaster ride has worn out any welcome possible."

As they slowly dematerialize, Clemens asks, "Walt, did you not notice what that man was wearing?"

"Err, no, I guess not. I was too involved with the moment. What was he wearing?"

"There were two mice holding hands on his shirt, not too unlike like the one we saw back a-ways. Seems your mouse has gotten around more than you'd imagine."

"To quote you: 'that's a humblization beyond my retention.'" Disney smirks, "I think it's the appropriate remark."

"I believe it to be accurately applied also."

The clearly distraught man watches the three disappear into a sandy vortex whirling skyward and blinks hard. "Well, I'll be! Ethel, I think I'm gonna stop drinking. I'm seeing things that ought not to be! This is too much for my genteel system."

....

While in the void, Disney asks again about the climactic events that have taken place, but Gabriel still stays silent. He senses something is amiss, "Sam, Eepia, I believe Mr. Toad's Wild Ride is not yet over."

Clemens asks, "What's a toad got to do with it?"

Eepia demurs, "I do not understand either. Can you give me a moment? I'll check with the crystal." She raises it to her forehead, "Oh, there is not a ride listed in this time frame. There was one, but it ended in 1998 and was replaced by a Winnie the Pooh." She hides a sly smile and asks, archly, "Does that mean our time is bare...ly up?"

Both men groan at her first foray into wordy witticisms and Disney exclaims, "Eepia, one confabulationist is enough for this trip!"

"Ouch, Walt, when have I ever lied to you? That hurts."

"Do you want me to ask the crystal, Mr. Disney? I'm sure it will most likely come up with more than a few occasions, even recently."

"Err, no Eepia, I think we know better, don't we, Sam? Or do you really want to know the number of times you've embellished the truth?"

"Humph, that would fill a volume all by itself." Sam realizes they are beginning to reappear. "Hold on, it seems as if my powers of attunement are providing us with another glimpse of something Walt still needs to know."

"Does that make you a seer, Sam?" Disney is intrigued.

"No, of course not, I just watch as the crystal stops its infernal humming and this elevator we're on is slowing us down. My achin' bones can tell."

"Well then, I guess we're here." Disney watches as the doors to Heaven's elevator they have been traveling in glide open and reveal their next destination.

....

Outside the elevator, they see bright sunlight and an open expanse of crystal-blue ocean. People mill about enjoying themselves, oblivious to the sudden appearance of an elevator on the sandy beach between two large boats.

The waves lapping the shore begin to dramatically recede and drain away into the normally calm, expansive and pristine bay.

No one seems to be bothered, or even notice it but them.

Eepia is alarmed, "Mr. Disney, the crystal says we are at a place called Phuket, Thailand, on December 26, 2004, at 9:45 a.m. It's Boxing Day. The crystal is already turning orange toward red and heating up. Do you want me to continue?"

The beach is dotted with numerous tourists and beach umbrellas. Small children are running and playing while their parents lie back on the hundreds of lawn chairs. Without warning, the tide suddenly disappears, leaving many boats literally dry docked.

People notice this and it feels ominous. Several scatter in multiple directions, yelling and screaming, while others are transfixed, not clearly understanding what is happening in the harbor. A total cacophony of international languages and cries erupts, and our travelers understand some of their abject pleadings as they resolve into phrases:

"Oh my God!"

"Where'd the water go?"

"It's a tsunami!"

"Run like bloody hell!"

The crystal glows white-hot in Eepia's hands, making it difficult to hold.

Disney yells, "Again?!" He moves to the elevator still on the beach and pushes several buttons at once. The doors remain open.

All eyes gaze in horror as the massive near-twenty-foot wave approaches.

Clemens is nearly frozen in place; he has never seen anything like it in his life. The huge wave draws nearer. The screaming, running mass of hysterical people has unnerved them utterly.

Disney is in near panic, "Gabriel, or whoever is in charge of getting us outta here, now is the time! Take us somewhere safe so I can catch my breath, PLEASE!"

Three terrified people in bathing suits run toward the elevator, their eyes glowing blank with panic … too late! The doors close. This is no longer a peaceful holiday and they are unable to make sense of why an elevator was on the each in the first place. The rushing, watery cataclysm engulfs them, and they pass into the greater unknown.

$$\infty$$

CHAPTER *18*

Disneyworld & Disneyland
2005

ℋOLDING his breath and eyes tightly shut, Disney fears for their safety. But then he senses a breath of both fresh and stale air, not sea air. It is eerily quiet.

He blinks, breathes, and grins. They're sitting in a log-style tram in the middle of a dark tunnel, and he recognizes exactly where they are: they're on the warm-up ride before the public is allowed in. Small mechanical dolls sing "It's a small world" as the tram rumbles slowly forward. Disney is moved to see it all again, and wipes a happy tear from his cheek.

Eepia is wide-eyed in wonderment as the magical experience unfolds.

Clemens is shocked. "Nobody is steering this contraption, at least I can't see the engineer. May I remind you we are wholly mortal right now?"

Disney laughs, "Relax, Sam. I remember this place: we are in Fantasyland, it's safe."

"Yeah, right! There are those who believe I spent the majority of my life here."

"You don't understand. This is a world I created with my imagination. I had a big dream that turned into reality. Being here … it means so much."

"You mean to inform me I'm riding through your noggin? That's what I'm supposed to swallow as fact?"

Disney stares at Clemens and then realizes there is a slight communication breakdown. "No-o-o, Sam, not at all. I built this amusement park: Disneyland. Another one was in the works in Florida, even bigger, some 28,000 planned acres of pure bliss and amusement. I wonder if there are still more to come."

"Humbly named you don't say … by yourself?"

Disney smiles, nods, almost embarrassed, "I also had lots of help, especially having to ride herd daily on a huge staff of workers."

Eepia is wholly captivated with the full-immersion Small World experience. Her eyes dance and her mouth moves with the words, which now are sung by Spanish dolls in their native language, as the tram moves through scenes from around the world.

"Sam, our little friend Eepia seems to be enthralled."

Clemens, however, is steadfastly appalled, "Bear in mind she also believes you and I are the epitome of great statesmen, so don't go judging your life's work by her reaction. I do have to admit, though, this is mildly entertaining."

"It is still here," Disney smiles proudly, "Feels like I never left."

"Pretty soon they will be switchin' to another song, right? I mean right away, right?"

Eepia sings loudly, "It's a small world after all," and louder still, in full-throated enthusiasm, "It's a small world after all!"

"No, Sam, not unless they changed it. As we go through each country, the dolls sing the same song in each native language. Originally, all of the little dolls in 'It's a Small World' were supposed to sing a different national anthem, and all at the same time. Thankfully, someone realized how annoying and horrible that would sound and the idea was abandoned. This is what it is. Relax and enjoy the ride."

"I see. Just how long is this ride and how many languages must we endure?"

Disney shrugs, "I seem to recall at least six or so, maybe more by now, whenever this now is."

Clemens rolls his eyes heavenward and frowns at Eepia's enthusiastic participation. "This has become an excruciatingly sweet experience. A person could die from terminal cuteness imprisoned on this wagon."

"You know, Sam, do you not notice there are no people on this ride? This must be the warmup as I thought. We might have the park completely to ourselves for a few monumental moments."

"You mean there is nobody here to rescue us from this ride? THAT is a troublesome thought."

Eepia continues singing unabashedly and is having a wonderful time. She is dressed in white twill pedal pushers, a pink knit tank top, and Birkenstock sandals.

The tram glides along and the track winds through tableaus from different countries. At last it slows down, signaling the end of the ride is near, much to Clemens' relief.

Once they've disembarked, Disney jumps up and out of the log-like tram and takes the lead. "Please, come this way, Sam. I have something to show you."

Clemens stops stubbornly and demands, "First tell me, does it sing?"

Disney laughs, shakes his head, and motions both to follow. His eyes dance with excitement; it is difficult for Sam and Eepia to keep up with him as he hurries along. As they forge ahead, the costumed character of Snow White walks by. Walt realizes the landscape is disorienting and his sense of direction doesn't quite work; are they in Disneyland?

Everything is different from his memory: the look, the rides, the landscaping, although not some of the people beginning to interact with the public. Disney realizes they are in the Florida park, not in California.

Eepia falls behind to admire the beautiful young woman in her costume. Slowly what she had been wearing changes to match Snow White's blue and white and black.

Clemens is startled by her change, shakes his head, and points to the tall figure of Pluto the dog ambling by. "I suppose we can be grateful you are more interested in the human species."

Disney is oblivious and urges, "Here! Over here! Hurry!"

Clemens walks faster and enters an area near water. He stops in his tracks at the sight of the Mark Twain Riverboat. A sign points to Tom Sawyer Island. Confused, he looks for answers. "Am I still going through a ride in your imagination? What is the answer for all of this?"

Disney struggles to speak, swallows hard, "I ... I told you that you have always been an influence on me. Eepia, do you think that you could help me out here? I am a bit overcome by this."

She raises the crystal to her forehead and recites, "We must go back to the days of Walt Disney's youth in Marceline, Missouri. His elementary school teacher chastised him for drawing flowers with smiles on their faces and carving his initials into his assigned desk. He was down by the Mississippi riverbank moping when an old man dressed in white walking along the bank paused to ask what the problem was. The man listened to the boy, bent over him and said, "Listen son, never grow up. Always let your imagination play. Don't be ruled by the adults' lack of enjoyment. I've never grown up and I don't plan to do it at this late date."

Clemens nods, remembers, beaming. "I remember ... that was you?"

Disney nods, "I was so thrilled by your support! You encouraged me when nobody had a lot of respect for or confidence in me. Of course, I had to have my own way and construct a tribute to one of the strongest mainstays of my life. You, my friend. It was because you encouraged me," sweeping his arms wide, "that all of this was possible." Disney can't do anything but grin, looks about in awe and amazement.

Sam looks about in awe and amazement. "I'm humbled ... deeply humbled. I didn't know."

A Disneyworld employee walks by, slows to a stop, sets down his broom and dustpan, and turns to look Clemens over. Obviously tickled he says, "How cool is this! A Mark Twain character! This is uber great!"

Clemens reaches into his pocket and pulls out a cigar, momentarily amazed at the quality of the stogie. Throwing back his head, he poses proudly under the employee's gaze. "This is a vanilla cigar, much nicer than I would share with my most intimate cronies. They do not economize on this tour, do they?"

Disney chuckles as he watches as the employee walk away without knowing who he'd actually encountered. He is euphoric. "These people seem as wholesome as when I last visited. This is a joy. A real heart-warmer. I'm deeply grateful my thoughts have taken us here. Yes, a perfect example of cause and effect at its finest. I need to remember to thank Gabriel for the fast rescue from possibly having to swim for our lives. Come to think of it, Eepia, do you know how to swim?"

"When we were back in the disco, Scott taught me a few steps to do the swim, or do you mean whether I know how to … is that sufficient?" She admires her reflection in the water and hums "It's a Small World" under her breath, then spontaneously breaks into boisterous singing, "It's a small world after all. It's a small world after all. It's a small world after all. It's a small, small world."

Sam narrows his eyes in mock anger, "This simple tune has taught me to abhor and detest cute little songs, and I shall dedicate my energy toward finding new and troublesome ways to dishonor anyone who could write like this."

Disney explains, "I seem to remember that the repetitiveness was cause for complaint. Let's board this steamboat before anyone notices us."

"I have an idea; we can always make believe that I am Mark Twain. I did it for a great deal of my life." They board Frontierland's Mark Twain Riverboat. Eepia is hesitant because it will be her first experience of needing sea legs, but she's already been exposed to other life-altering events, has come through them fine, and has grown up exponentially in the process.

"I wish it were after dark." Disney looks around, "Tinkerbell flies across the park and magnificent fireworks displays light up the sky; at least they did at Disneyland. Here, I don't know as much yet. The entertainment is supposed to be consistent and wonderful. It is all still exhilarating for me."

Clemens does not speak. He is feeling deeply emotional as he continues to move upward to the top deck; he looks across the water. "Never thought I would experience being a riverboat captain again. Forgot how powerful a feelin' it is for a man."

The Goofy character approaches Clemens with a friendly demeanor. Through sign language, he signals his approval of the Mark Twain character, a new personality on the boat; Clemens thoroughly enjoys the attention.

Throngs of people begin to pour aboard, and many are wearing golden mouse ears in honor of the park's 50th anniversary, both surprising and pleasing to Disney.

Clemens smiles broadly when a lady approaches him with an autograph book; she poses next to him for a picture. He looks at Eepia's crystal waiting for it to glow red.

Nothing happens.

Clemens is mystified, "Watch closely, I'm writing, "My very best to you and yours."

The crystal doesn't even flicker.

He cannot understand it. The woman moves to stand nearer the Goofy character and has him pose and sign her book, too.

Clemens is totally dumbfounded.

The delighted mother is wild with joy. She looks back over her shoulder to address her partner, "Honey, the kids will be so jealous that I had my picture taken with Goofy!"

Clemens can't fathom this, "This is humblization beyond my retention. That woman cherished the autograph of an oversized dog, with a possible malady to boot, over my own signature. When do we leave? I thought as soon as my signature appeared on a paper we would be transported."

Disney has developed greater understanding because the travelers have passed through many events, some nightmarish, some not—like this one. He speaks from that awareness to Sam, "Only—apparently—if the person reading it believes it is indeed you. These folks think you are an actor, and me as well, I guess."

Eepia leans on the rail, looking out across the water. Her singing has encouraged a following. The melody surrounds one and all as people on the boat and dockside join in, singing, "It's a small world after all..."

Walt is waxing nostalgic, "I needed to know what I had created survived my death. I don't need to know more than this, 'cept how my favorite horse on King Arthur's Carousel, "Jingles," is holding up. But ..."

Clemens gestures at the Goofy character in full costume and persuades him to come closer. He motions for him to bend down to hear a secret. As he does, Clemens lifts the dog's ear—and promptly disappears. Simultaneously, so do Eepia and Disney.

Goofy turns in all directions to find Twain. Shaking his head, he stumbles in confusion down the ramp to exit the boat while "When You Wish Upon a Star" plays on the dock.

Disney is clearly amused. He realizes his thinking and dreaming have created something wonderful for everyone who visits the park to experience their childhood dreams. He concentrates on wishing to see where he first envisioned, then built, his creation.

It happens in a flash of golden light.

....

Disney, emotionally spellbound, looks around gawking at the park, then notices the 50th anniversary logos above numerous ride entrances. "Golly, it's been 50 years since this first came into being. That makes it mid to late July, 2005."

Eepia is still humming while Clemens huffs and puffs along, somewhat startled that they are elsewhere, yet their surroundings are familiar. "Walt, what are you up to now? We seem to be around similar contraptions, yet they are different. Are you still playin' with my noggin?"

Disney is delighted to have arrived at the Carousel and unsettled to see a sign posted on the saddle of his personal favorite horse, Jingles:

RESERVED FOR THE RETURN OF IMAGINEER WALT DISNEY. KEEP OFF!

He quickly advances and removes it, then sits atop his steed teary-eyed.

An obnoxious youngster approaches, wearing too-tight shorts, his little belly sticking out from under an equally too-small t-shirt with a Star Wars logo, and his Dodgers baseball cap on backward. "Hey, mister, this ride is for kids only. I'm next!"

He tries unsuccessfully to pull Disney off.

"Wait your turn." Disney is emphatic, unwilling to abbreviate his nostalgic moments. "This is my time on Jingles. And if you're lucky, maybe, just maybe, my horse will let you sit atop it, but don't count on it. Your attitude is not worthy of the ascended altitude."

He realizes many changes have occurred during his absence. "I've heard it said, 'Change is inevitable, growth is optional.' My Disneyland idea has grown and prospered far beyond my vision." He continues to survey his surroundings and sees the narrow-gauge railroad train with Lilly Bell, his favorite caboose named after Lillian, his wife.

He is momentarily sad. "Oh to be back here in the flesh. What will it be like? What should I decide…?"

The youngster interrupts Disney and insists, "My mama paid good money for me to be here, now get off!"

"Young man," Disney looks at him sternly, "do you know the words 'please' and 'thank you'?"

"That's none of your business. I'll call the cops and tell them you're trying to get me to go on a ride with you if you don't do what I say."

Clemens is close now and quickly suggests, "He's a feisty two-legged ornery little critter don't you think? Maybe someone with authority can get to the seat of his problem with a switch of sorts. It's been known to alter one's psychological perspective about things."

Disney hands the youngster the RESERVED sign. "Here. Give this to someone in charge and see what they say. Now watch closely."

Sparkles dance around the two men and nearby Eepia as she sees what is about to occur. The crystal is glaring redly in her hands.

The youngster is flabbergasted by the sight of three adults disappearing into a funnel-like void right in front of him. "Mama!"

....

Meanwhile, not far away, an older woman is walking with several young-sters in tow. They stop to watch the commotion unfold on the carousel; the woman is the little Plaster girl all grown up. Are the children her own?

She tells them, "Jimmy, Misty, and Trudy, this carousel was one of the first rides I ever took when I came here the very first visit. It was exciting and such a happy time. I remember I couldn't wait to get back home to Livingston and take out my big drawing tablet that I got for a birthday, where I practiced drawing characters and flowers with happy faces."

She sees a distinguished older man on the carousel handing a sign, taken from one of the horses, to a defiant youngster. Close to him is a white-haired gentleman puffing enthusiastically on a cigar in open defiance of the non-smoking rule while on the Magic Kingdom's grounds.

She considers going over and speaking to him about putting out the foul-smelling thing, but decides to rein in her impulse instead and leave it to an employee or someone willing to approach him. A young lady next to him is holding an object that is glowing bright crimson, then a flash of light surrounds them.

A moment later she sees only space where the three were, and wonders aloud, "How can that be? I just saw them distinctly. Is that a new attraction to this land of magic at Disneyland?"

The three children are oblivious to Sherry's commentary, far more inter-ested in holding on to their mouse balloons and their mouse-ear hats on their tiny heads. Each was holding a kind of camera and so fascinated with it, play-ing and pushing little keys, they were ignoring what was around them. "Well kids, if you aren't interested in seeing any more of this special place, I guess we can all go back to the hotel and you can go swimming, maybe play some miniature golf, or spend some quality time with me, your auntie?"

The three nod their heads in unison and Jimmy, the eldest, asks politely, "Can we have some pizza, Aunt Sherry, before we go back?" He looks up in anticipation, "And maybe have an ice cream sundae?"

She laughs, "Yes, yes of course we can. Let's head back to the Main Street anyway; it's much too early for the Parade of Lights."

∞

CHAPTER 19

Hurricane Katrina

DISNEY, Clemens, and Eepia quickly realize their whirlwind journey through time and space has met reality head-on. They have arrived somewhere yet identified, but it's pouring torrential rain and the winds are howling like a banshee alerting an entire village about imminent death. Disney, his confusion and concern for their safety growing every moment, says, "I sense where we are is neither Disneyland nor Disneyworld. Where are we now, Eepia?"

The onslaught of the howling and vicious wind are nothing compared to the inundating volume of rainwater that pours down on them, as if the sky has opened, unlike anything either Disney or Clemens encountered while on Earth. It's increasingly difficult to walk, let alone stand upright. Eepia exclaims, "Is this is what it's like to be raining buckets full?"

Sam counters with another query, "Did I ever tell you about when it rained cats and dogs?"

"Sam, now is neither the time nor place for one of your long-winded explanations, no matter how entertaining you might be. We need to secure ourselves a safer place, first and foremost. If time permits while we wait out this cataract, then yes, enlighten us."

"Oh, all right. After all, I'm here as part of your experience, Walt. How and why would you ever think up this one anyway?"

The storm seems to have taken on a personality of its own, and the increasing wind groans and wails. Every pelting raindrop is like a needle drilling into exposed flesh, propelled sideways with terrible force. The driving deluge makes it nearly impossible for anyone to see even a few yards ahead.

They struggle along the deserted street, the water still cascading down in torrents and wave after wave of furious wind rattling the overhead signs—even attached to storefronts—as if readying themselves to set sail to parts unknown. It felt like they were riding the storm rudderless, in utterly unfamiliar territory, and to make things worse, the water churning down in waves was up to their ankles. They might be swept off their feet at any moment. Even Gene Kelly might've paused before trying to sing and dance in this violent weather.

The mounting fierceness of tempest assaults their senses, robbing them of any stability. Should they go where the storm was directing them? Their trajectory is unknown, and they are in the depths of despair. While slogging through inches of salt water on the street, suddenly a large garbage can careers toward them on a collision course. Disney grabs Eepia just in time as it hurtles by, missing her by mere inches!

She gasps, sputtering through a mouthful of water, "Oh thank you, I couldn't see where I was heading or what to do."

Upset and cantankerous, Sam pipes up, "Were your eyes glued shut to yer eyelids?"

A desperate squealing sound overtakes their conversation, and a potbellied pig washes by them. Disney cannot resist such a stellar opportunity for spontaneous campiness and wordplay. He looks squarely into Clemens's contorted face, points, and archly declares, "See that? That's hogwash!"

Thoroughly soaked and wobbly on his feet, Sam growls, "I defy anyone to remain an upstanding citizen. Walt, what did you say to Gabriel to endanger our very existence, whether it be surreal, physical, or otherwise? Was it anything like 'When pigs fly!'?"

Even in peril, he retains his inimitable sense of jocularity.

Looking around through eyes open to mere slits, Disney tries his best to spy anything resembling possible safety. Every cell vibrated with an alertness he has never before experienced. He must get them to security and soon! But where? Where are they?

Eepia, shivering violently, is exasperated, "I have bumps all over my arms and legs—will I explode or fly away like Tinker Bell, Mr. Disney?"

The storm lashes into them at a fever pitch. Through the pandemonium surrounding them words cut through the din—not spoken by Disney, Clemens, or Eepia: "Get yer asses over here now!"

Following that mysterious voice, they move toward it as swiftly as the tumult would allow. By sheer will and iron determination, the three travelers navigate the sideways blasts of wind and rain. The voice urges, "Hurry up! I can't keep the door open any longer! It's ready to come off its hinges iffen you don't get here in the next three seconds!" A man wedging open the door of a storefront is gesturing wildly, holding a loudspeaker to his mouth and waving his free arm back and forth frantically to draw their attention.

At a seeming snail's pace, they churn forward toward the doorway, believing it might be their only chance at safety. An earsplitting crackle, immediately followed by an intense blinding light, strikes right behind them, where they had been nanoseconds before.

The man in the doorway yells again, "Don't you three know any better? It's a category five and yer about to get blown away iffen you don't move! Get yerselves in here now!"

Panicked Disney looks from Eepia to Clemens. Despite the melee, Eepia somehow has accessed the Akashic record crystal and her words drill the desperation of their predicament into their minds, "We are in the middle of the French Quarter of New Orleans, and Hurricane Katrina is arriving. What's a hurricane?"

Another loud crackle announces the storm's mounting fury, and several streaks of lightning hurtle to earth. One strikes a power pole all too near them, and the transformer explodes in a dazzling and terrifying display.

The startling hiss and crackle and acrid odor make Eepia scream, "Oh golly! Help us, Gabriel!" She jumps around frantically, unable to contain her fear in the ferocious wind and rain, and tosses the crystal to Disney. He fumbles to catch it, but the spinning, hurtling crystal slips from Walt's slick hands and tumbles end over end to the flooded street toward a choked storm drain. A split-second later, the sky lights up and another lightning bolt blazes down and strikes it squarely, obliterating the crystal into thousands of razor-sharp shards.

Total blackout!

Eepia screams desperately, "Help!"

Disney's voice rings with horror, "What is happening? Is this the end of life as we know it?"

Clemens shouts into the darkness, "Now you've gone and done it, Slick; we're dead fer certain!"

. . . .

Suddenly—no more rain, no wind, no flood, only a gentle upward movement swaying back and forth, rocking them. In the luminescent space, they see and grab hold of a railing along the walls about waist-high. It's dry. Clemens is first to comment, calm now, "I can earnestly say, this here elevator is a most welcome sight."

"Thank you for our lives, Gabriel." Disney is both humble and grateful. "You came through in the nick of time." Beaming like a parent at Eepia, proud of her exponential growth, he adds, "And thank you, Eepia, for your fervent plea—why did you, anyway?"

She takes a deep, cleansing breath, "The crystal told me that, had we stayed where we were and gone to that storefront, we faced ... certain death. Inside was a bunch of marauding thieves and cutthroats ready to take full advantage of us without regard for ending human lives."

Disney gulps and heaves a ragged sigh. He speaks with obvious discomfort, "Oh my, that would have indeed fouled up any thoughts of returning to Earth in a timely fashion."

"Walt, you coulda died twice! That woulda been a record of sorts," Clemens remarks. "Say now; maybe I might have written a scenario or sumthin' akin to it." Clemens muses aloud: "I'll have to check my record books about death-defying dealings with the devil's own."

"Ahem," Gabriel's unmistakable voice cuts in. "You were about to become an illogical and logistical nightmare that even God himself could not have dreamed up. We're nearing Heaven's landing zone, and once you three have dried off, you'll find clean clothes for you and some hot chocolate with marshmallows and whipped cream to warm your insides."

Ebullient again, Eepia's eyes dance with excitement, "Any chances for some sprinkles on top too?"

Gabriel's voice is warm and understanding, "Yes, dear sweet Eepia, sprinkles will be available."

"Oh goody!"

The elevator slows to a gentle stop and they disembark. Disney wipes his brow, realizing the inevitable next step, "Gabriel, after this last episode, I suppose it's decision-making time, yes?"

"How about yes for an answer. You know where my office is. See you soon."

∞

CHAPTER 20

It's Almost Time to Decide

HEAD Angel Gabriel sits behind his desk in Heaven's Waiting Room, discussing the next step for Disney with Walt, Eepia, and Sam. They are abruptly interrupted by a knock at the door. Both Disney and Clemens swivel around in their free-floating chairs to face the unexpected visitor.

The ornate double doors slide sideways soundlessly, and Steve Jobs enters. He stops in his tracks to find the office already occupied by Clemens, Disney, and Eepia as she sways back and forth in her favorite floating swing. She wears a beguiling vibrant lavender robe and her hair cascades down to her shoulders.

Jobs' eyes widen in surprise, then recognition, as his mind flashes back to seeing them at the Menlo Park garage sale when he was developing the first home computer. "Well, I'll be!" He exclaims happily. "It wasn't my imagination, it was the three of you after all! I was so focused on improving computing I didn't think much of it … until now. This makes better sense."

Clemens is first to acknowledge their presence, "My good man … I'm not denying or confirming it was us you think you saw at an earlier date and time and place … but we have been touring about, catchin' up on things important to Walt's decision-making abilities. So now I'm pondering, why did we meet you and, even more importantly, why are you here? Shouldn't you be back workin' on your newest contraptions?"

Steve is beside himself with joy, "Mr. Clemens, don't you know? You gave me an apple with a bite taken out of it and that launched our product name."

"Well, how thoughtful; your justifiable consideration humbles me … not that I'm not deserving of your praise after all. Thank you, lad. When did you form this product if I may so inquire?"

"We formed our company—called Apple by the way—on April Fools' Day, 1976." Jobs laughs at the absurdity. "Steve Wozniak and I created a new computer circuit board in the garage during that garage sale. Our third partner, Ron Wayne, was there too, but he left us soon afterward."

"Now, that's what I call that a real hoot! April Fools' Day you say? You seem to have a knack for play, am I not right?"

Jobs smiles knowingly but says nothing. He looks around the shimmering, bejeweled surroundings and the lighting mesmerizes him: it appears angelic to him and not resemble any he's seen on earth.

Disney is intrigued, "What became of this company of yours, Mr. Jobs?"

"Boast if you must, lad." Clemens instructs, a self-amused smile on his face, "You are among friends who tell only the truth here."

Eepia's eyes widen at this pronouncement; she's seen first-hand how the old curmudgeon snickers at sidestepping the truth when it's convenient, and chides him. "Mr. Clemens, you know better, shame on you."

Clemens' self-serving equivocation fuels his choice to disregard her admonishment. He blusters, "This is the place for reconciling such matters of importance anyway, right, Gabriel?"

"Correct," Gabriel concedes, "Go on, please, Steve, we are all eager to hear."

Jobs begins, "My success came at a great personal cost. The emotional and physical sacrifices I made along the way finally brought me here," he points out a nearby window, "not there anymore." He is both tranquil and melancholy. "Once we launched the personal computer, the industry took off like wildfire and a whole host of ideas bubbled up in me.

"I can say I was helpful in creating a few things that have helped humankind when they were used constructively. Apple personal computers are now staple tools in schools, businesses, and homes worldwide."

They listen attentively and get comfortable to hear the tale. Disney and Clemens soon return to lounging in the floating chairs, and Eepia stands near the swing, remarking almost to herself, "Yes indeed, it is a small, small world."

Jobs continues, "Struggles between distinct parts of the company were resolved after I was booted out—I'd run it my way because in my mind, it was better to be a pirate than to be in the navy, but the CEO didn't agree. I was devastated, but I started over because I loved what I did. I returned to Apple some ten years later and was not merely a visionary, I learned how to be a businessman." He pauses. "Apple bought NeXT, which I'd also founded, and brought me back on as CEO. Life got much more hectic for me personally after that, and my physical health deteriorated as a result."

"Now don't all that sound familiar?" Clemens looks to Disney, then turns to Jobs, "Go ahead lad, we're all ears. I'm certain there's a bit more to the story than meets the eye, right?"

"Yes, sir, most definitely," he says, saddened by the memory, "my eating habits were not based on the healthiest decisions, and I sank into a downward spiral that ultimately cost me my life. Simply put, I was too tired from an eight-year battle with a particularly insidious cancer. I've come through the hell of it and being here, with you … well, it seems I've been moving toward the high-water mark in spite of myself."

His self-deprecatory comment tickles everyone's funny bone, even Eepia's, and they giggle appreciatively. "The illness ravaged my body beyond any degree I could imagine, and I simply gave in—now I'm ready to begin again. So here I stand in this magnificent office in front of you. What's next?"

"For one," responds Gabriel in friendly support, "allow me to take you to a place where you can regenerate. We will review your life's purpose and then decide on when, where, and what to do next, perhaps rather like the journey Walt has recently completed."

"Yes, circumspection is wholly encouraged—and none too soon, I might add." Clemens will never change; his ego demands he get his last licks in. "Walt will get to look through his viewing contraption for a bit before he makes any final decisions, right Gabe?"

Gabriel declares, "I have just decided to put it up on the macro screen for all of us to see. Watch carefully now, so you don't miss anything." He glides swiftly to the console at his desk. Everyone finds a soft cloud-like cushion to sit on and settles in, ready and willing to watch intently while a montage of scenes from the past fifty years of history rolls before them at lightning speed. It slows down to highlight the times and places that Eepia, Clemens, and Disney interacted with earth's occupants, and includes a visit to Michael Jackson's Neverland Ranch and George Lucas selling Lucasfilm to The Walt Disney Company in 2012.

It visibly shakes Clemens when he sees Ellen de Generes receive the Mark Twain Prize. She mentions she had never read any of his works. He is speechless.

The montage ends and Gabriel asks, "So, Walt, are you ready to decide what comes next for you?"

"First, if you will, explain to me why we experienced such proximity to so many earth-shaking moments and horrendous tragedies?"

Gabriel reflects for a moment, then reveals, "Walt, as you well know from being on earth, calamities happen during the natural course of events. During your time there and up until 1960, major upheavals occurred that nobody heard about or saw, other than those immediately involved. The sphere of our known earth has become smaller, directly because of technological advancements. Humanity is now able to view things as they happen and, as a result, man's awareness has become more influenced by the foibles and pitfalls of human nature and man's direct influence on global conditions—warranted or not. Despite all of that, inspired thinkers and dreamers have yet to figure out what comes next. Your particular situation is in such a category. Nothing is sacrosanct. You've been shielded from the last five decades of global changes; we here in Heaven thought you needed a jump start before making your impending decision."

"That reminds me of the proverbial shotgun approach," Clemens interjects, "like having a Remington 1900 double-barreled in the hands of the pregnant bride's father at a wedding, and you are the groom tied to the podium up there with the officiant!"

"Yes Sam, more or less like that." Gabriel acknowledges with a smile, then returns to the business at hand. "Back to what I was saying, the events we chose for you to experience were meant to exemplify man's inhumanity to itself. Now, kindly see what's happening to you back on earth." Gabriel waves his hands and the familiar, sparkling waves of imminent teleportation begin. "Off you three go!" They shimmer out of sight.

Jobs inquires, "Sir, you mentioned a place for review and regeneration—R&R—to examine my purpose, if in life I hit the proverbial bull's eye, or missed it (and perhaps by how much), and said something about deciding about my next journey, perhaps similar to Disney's visits to earth. If it's up to me, I think I'll pass on that. Maybe I could consider mentoring or counseling about up-and-coming technical ideologies; seems that has been a forte of mine. So, if you would, I am ready to do just that... it's what the doctor's ordered, right?"

Gabriel has been preoccupied by thoughts of his charges' latest experiences at the lab, but drags his attention back to the present. "Yes, but of course! Forgive me, Steve, for not attending to you until this moment. As you may surmise, things are afoot with Disney, and we wish to help him make the best decisions possible for his highest outcome."

"I can certainly understand that," Jobs is feeling somewhat anxious about his impending opportunity and being able to review his own Akashic record, because he doesn't really know what it entails. He spent most of his life living by his wit and intelligence and less from his heart. "Are you going to show me the way, or do I need or have an escort, or is there a particular colored line to for me to follow?"

Gabriel laughs at this last image, "No, Steve, no yellow brick road for you to follow. Just go through the door opening on your left; it leads where you will find what you seek. Go with my blessings. And thank you for sharing about how your life-style choices contributed to your early demise. I believe Eepia is taking all this learning into consideration before her first journey in the flesh. Not that it influences Clemens, however; his being here has been an interesting experience for all of us! At least he has had a meritorious journey with Walt and might even "write sumthin' down" thus perpetuating his felicitous talent for the written word."

CHAPTER *21*

Back on Earth

THEY arrive at a lab in the same cryonics facility where Disney's body has been stored since 1966, remodeled and updated since then. A clutch of medical personnel wearing white lab coats and colorful scrubs work feverishly and use the most current and technologically advanced monitors and medical equipment. They busily surround Disney's lifeless body like a swarm of bees around their queen.

In a nearby corner, Disney's, Eepia's, and Clemens' semitransparent figures huddle together, whispering. Disney is amazed to see his mortal body hooked up to so many wires leading to a dizzying array of apparatuses and gadgets either positioned nearby or attached to it, ready to indicate the body's status on multiple screens and portable laptops.

He struggles to adjust to the distinctly sterile environment while recognizing a future-changing major decision awaits, and whispers to his companions, "Well, from the looks of things, I guess it is getting to be time to choose whether I stay or go...."

"Walt, my boy," Sam offers encouragingly, "looks like they are ready for just about anything. I've never seen so much paraphernalia and gadgetry in my life. God only knows what they can do or not do. Hmmm, what if I were to sidle over close to one or two of them, just to see what kinda reaction I could muster from them? Whatcha think? Yes, no? I'd like to see these hovering buzzards scamper about..."

"Absolutely not!" Disney whispers fiercely. He is adamant. "Stay put! And if you don't, I'll personally haunt you until the end of days! This is MY TIME and no one's gonna ruin it ... unless it's me."

"Walt, breathe easy, I was only kidding. I was just trying to lighten the mood around this-here mausoleum-like atmosphere." His eyes well up with tears. "Sorry iffen I offended you." Clemens pleads with Eepia. "Maybe you can assure him I was only acting like my usual self-serving self?"

Her straightforward stare is disarming, "After all this time, your sense of timing is decidedly slipping, Mr. Clemens. Can't you tell when it's time to leave well enough alone?"

Clemens hangs his head in remorse.

He appeals to Disney, "Can you ever forgive me for this indiscretion? For the record, it's jest cuz that's what I've been doing with you since you first arrived back yonder, and I can't fathom what Heaven will be like with you back here, iffen that's the final choice you make. I suppose now is as good a time as any to apologize for shorting your allotted time through the last fifty or so years."

"You? Sorry for what?" Disney thinks about it for several long seconds. "I saw, felt, and heard enough; even had a few laughs on and with you. This simply is not an easy decision for me to make. And I'm sorry too, for jumping on you like that. My nerves are a bit frayed."

Eepia asks, still the innocent, "What do frayed nerves look like?" Her current outfit befits the occasion: she wears an all-white, simple angelic robe. "I wish to thank you for letting me go with you both. I have learned so much, and I can truly say I will never be the same. From what I have learned about the two of you, when there is a decision to make, whether you make one or not, that too is a decision. I still have more to learn."

"To my surprise," Clemens snips, "I learned a good amount, too—mostly about myself."

"Sam, what did you learn," asks Disney, "if it's not too personal?"

"Now how is it going to be anything but personal if it is about me?"

"Good point, Sam! I need to explain, I think. I'm hoping to make this a quick visit, in case I do decide to go back into this time frame and a physical reality. I deeply care a lot about you and would miss you. I'll wager you know, from past experiences, I do know how to delay a thing or two."

Clemens is touched by the emotional display and disclosure, "Remember when I told you how much death—the fear of it—ruled my life, unbeknownst to me?"

"Yes."

"I used to worry about the void Livvy and Susie faced. They were so vital one day and gone the next. It was only after my own death that I understood. You play either one role or the other. I didn't want to upset my loved ones, so I stayed the same song-and-dance person. Ultimately, I was alone during my transition. Wish I could've shared it."

Disney glides weightlessly around the room, glancing here and there at the sterile hospital-like environment and the various monitors as he responds to Sam's revelation. "It was the same for me. As you said, we experience death alone, no matter how many folks are present. I suppose that is the way it will always be. I couldn't take anything with me except my thoughts and personality."

"Why?" Clemens asks. "What makes that the rule? I think a celebration of life is warranted. Don't you agree how wonderful it would have been to hear people share old memories and allude to the good things our association meant to their lives? What a great tribute it would be to know your life made a difference."

Eepia is suddenly teary-eyed and sniffs, "I was with you both for only a short while, and you have made a significant difference in me."

Clemens reaches over and gently squeezes her shoulder with true affection, "Young lady, whether you realize it or not, you made a difference everywhere you went."

Disney reminisces, "Going back to my two Disneyland parks and seeing how my dream was, err, still being cherished, maintained, and even a bit embellished—that was wonderful. But was it enough?"

"Enough for whom?" Clemens pipes up and points, "For you to decide to resurrect in this here body? For you to decide you'd made enough of a difference already, despite all them health issues you had going agin you?"

"Was it, or better yet, is it enough for me to make the final decision?" Walt ponders a counterproductive thought: "Building the Disneyland theme parks is a cherished memory I shall always be comfortable with. And if I do go back, will I be comfortable enough to rest on my laurels?"

"Certainly not!" Clemens is unwavering, "I cannot imagine you sittin' anywhere for long, even at your special stopover place above that firehouse on Main Street to watch the parade go by. On that premise, my friend, you will always want to be in the midst of it. You've never been one to sit back and watch; no siree, you're too impatient and yer eye twitches when you're excited. I've seen you work tirelessly, never taking a moment out to stop what you're doing, even if where we've been doesn't have sleeping arrangements other than an occasional cloud, or cafeteria."

Disney is taken aback, "My eye twitches?"

Clemens chuckles, "That's because no one has ever been with you long enough to watch you as carefully as I."

Gabriel arrives and joins in, "As a matter of fact, Sam, I believe you are right about that. I hadn't noticed."

Not one to be out from the spotlight for any length of time, Clemens declares joyfully, "As for me, seeing the Mark Twain Riverboat so many years after my death, was absolutely, positively astoundin'!" He slaps his thigh in gleeful wonder, "I do believe that somehow my feeble attempts to put ideas into written words did make a difference. Why don't we train people how to deal positively with the inevitable? I've learned through my years of traveling and such that pleasing everyone is impossible, but the ability to piss 'em off is much easier. I made an earnest effort in later years to maximize my talents in the latter. Even you, Walt, you made a difference I'd say, unequivocally."

Disney focuses his attention on the activity around his physical body, no longer listening to Sam's eloquent and conciliatory words. Clemens is sensitive to this internal wrestling match and glides easily across the floor to hover near him.

"Sam, I feel so alienated from this process," Disney says, staring intently at the form on the bed, "That can't be me under that sheet, can it?"

With a twinkle in his eye, Clemens observes, "Ya know, Walt, I once saw a dog be brought back from Hades' door, a condition not so different from this. It, too, had been frozen. Fallen into ice water, if I have my facts right."

"I can't believe you are doing this," Disney exclaims, incredulous to be lumped in with a Mark Twain dog story, "… now!"

Immune, Clemens continues, "The old gal who owned the consarned animal sat right down on it, sobbing as though her heart was practically done for. Somehow that stiff ol' mutt, which never earned a meal in its life, began to take its first shudderin' breaths, whimperin' sumpthin fierce, probably due to bein' squeezed by and bein' under the lady's immensity."

Disney smiles with adoration and raises his palms in mock defeat. "You know that no matter what I decide to do, or not, I will never be able to top the dog story! Not even when we filmed 'Old Yeller'."

"Anyway," Sam says with exaggerated patience, determined to complete his tale of a tail just so, "as I was sayin'… The old gal who owned the consarned animal sat right on it, sobbing as though her heart was practically done for. Somehow…" his eyes twinkled, "that old dog began to breathe. Like to have sent that ol' gal into the clenches of the Other Side, it scared her so when the dog yelped to get her off him."

Eepia and Disney laugh aloud at this latest yarn. Several medical personnel hear giggling somewhere and are thoroughly surprised. They look at one another dumbfounded, and one scratches his head involuntarily, grimaces at his action, and immediately leaves to resterilize his hands before returning to his intense scrutiny of the lifeless body.

The three disembodied spirits snicker, acquiescing in readiness for the story's coda, and Clemens continues unabashedly, "Didn't take long for it to resume its lifelong habits of eating, lying around, growling periodically to bluff a person into thinking it was one to be reckoned with—and sleeping. Sleeping was its best talent."

Head Angel Gabriel turns to the bed where Disney's inert form lies. "Walt, my friend, it is time for your decision. Have you made it yet?"

"Not so you'd notice," he admits. Disney shakes his head from side to side, "this is impossible! What if I'm not ready?"

"Nothing is impossible, Mr. Disney," Eepia responds, "not for Gabriel, the heavenly team, and certainly not for you, the One and Only Original Imagineer."

Understanding and concern weigh heavily on Disney; they register on his drooping shoulders. "I realize that, I do. But I have left so much undone!" He points upward and at the floor, "both there and here."

Gabriel smiles and inquires, "Like what?"

Walt takes a breath, "Like that little girl in Livingston, California—the one I was observing when all of this started. She needed some guidance. I wanted to be sure she received it."

"OK, I see." Gabriel asks, "What would you do or have done?"

"As I see it, she is a gifted cartoonist. Maybe beyond that, maybe a naturally talented child. I would try to impress upon her mind to use her imagination and try different creative avenues, like illustrating her book reports or social studies papers. She would not only learn, but she might also gain the respect of her peers. And possibly so much more."

Gabriel pats Disney on the shoulder and nods agreement. "Good to know you approve. Everyone come with me back to my office for a moment."

Their forms dissolve into a flurry of little stars, unnoticed by the physicians and medical personnel looking deeply into tech manuals, figuring their best course to bring about Walter Elias Disney's re-emergence.

∞

CHAPTER 22

Gabriel's Office—Again

THE four rematerialize in Gabriel's bright inner sanctum and immediately see his office has been remodeled for the umpteenth time. Now, a gigantic screen hovers with no visible support in the middle of the room. The sun's rays filter through a variety of panels, mirrors, and window-like openings in the semiopaque, permeable walls. It's as if they breathe on their own, and have an intelligence that disseminates kaleidoscopic patterned rays of light. No one need use sunglasses.

Gabriel speaks, "I invite you to look at some images though my personal viewing scope. Sit back on any cloud-cushion that seems comfortable to you, relax, and enjoy the view."

They seat themselves obediently on the nearest puff of cloud, which transforms promptly to fit each one's size and shape. The gigantic screen zeroes in on the young cartoonist they had just been discussing. In the bottom left corner of the screen, a time stamp indicates the year, 1957, when the young girl was enrolled in a junior high school reading classroom in Chico, California.

"Precisely as you said, Walt, that is what we impressed upon her, and at this very moment she is drawing Tom Sawyer as he painted his picket fence. She will be just fine, and so much more than you can possibly imagine."

Disney is pleased and clasps his hands in a winning gesture. "That's grand, a job well done. She has learned a valuable lesson: use your talents, even if they haven't been recognized by anyone else yet."

"Gabe did more than undermine your argument, I'd say he blew a large hole in it. So," Clemens asks, "what else concerns you about staying or going, Walt?"

"OK. Do you think it is possible? Did I really make any difference?"

"You're beginning to be an embarrassment," Clemens whispers into Disney's ear, "It ain't what you don't know that gets you into trouble. It's what you know for sure what just ain't so."

Sam then addresses Gabriel, "Sir, he is not a novice ... he is decidedly far beyond amateur status."

"It is entirely up to you, Walt," Gabriel counsels, "and always has been. Surely you have known that from the very start of your fifty-year sojourn. If I failed to help you understand at the beginning of your journey, I'll say it specifically now: you interact in ways that touch people's soul-essence. What happens next is up to the person to do what is appropriate for them. You, Walter Elias Disney, have been a visionary, an emissary of sorts—not a missionary and not to be confused as one."

Gabriel glances toward Eepia, "Speaking of decision-making, young lady, I heard from on high that it's nearly time for you to contemplate moving forward too. Any thoughts about that?"

"Hmmm, yes," she replies, "I do believe it's time for me to take on 'an adventure of unimagined magnitude'... I've been appropriately tutored."

"So much has changed during these past decades," Disney mumbles under his breath as he watches a current timeline on the large viewing screen. He scans the display as children play with toy laser guns. Other kids are watching something on a small, handheld rectangular screen. They notice a now-familiar emblem—an apple missing a bite—on the back of many of the objects. Clemens points to the logo and smiles, remembering what Jobs had said about the Apple logo, and chooses to hold his tongue for the time being.

Gabriel is genuinely concerned for Disney, "What frightens you, my friend?"

"Everything! It is all so different. If I am right, the Mouseketeers would be beyond middle-aged. I can't imagine Cubby, Karen, Bobby, and Annette retired now, or altogether departed from life. Are any of them here, or have I been too involved with looking through rose-colored glasses?"

Sam coughs, "You will never know how much I hesitate to ask, but ... what is a Mouseketeer?"

Gabriel presses a console button on his desk. The massive image transfers to a viewing window behind Gabriel's ornate desk. Disney shakes his head at Clemens and a "you will never understand" look and turns to the display on the wall, which focuses first on 1980, the 25th reunion that Annette hosted and 31 of the 39 original members attended. The next image is from 2010 at the Livingston High School 1965 reunion with Doreen Tracey and Sharon Baird in person.

"What?" Disney is totally taken aback, "Their reunion was where little Sherry Plaster—the one I was so concerned about—attended school?"

"An amazing coincidence, don't you think, Walt?" asks Clemens.

"There is no such thing as coincidence, as you all readily know." Gabriel reminds them, "There is Cause and Effect. This is another example of unintended consequence; they seem to surround us daily and, when one looks deeper, everything is connected to the larger scheme of things. One must look through their own eyes rightly."

Eepia comments, "I learned about that before deciding to venture out as a new soul. From my previously ethereal viewpoint, I could connect a few dots that previously seemed disconnected; I saw they weren't. Art, science, and religion are interrelated, part of the Universal triune. Maybe someday scientists will be able to see more clearly, once they look outside their comfortable-but-confining boxes. They seem to be holding up the process."

She looks over at Disney and says lovingly, "I see nothing wrong with growing older and wiser. Thanks to you, Mr. Disney, I did it in short order, and love it. Think of what they must have learned during all that time."

Disney's face brightens in a fatherly smile, "Yes, you have grown considerably since hooking up with the likes of us."

Gabriel moves to stand next to Disney, to support him through his confusion. Winking at Clemens, Gabriel explains, "Walt, referring now to your issues and concerns: you did get here a little earlier than planned, due to some scheduled and unscheduled take-offs from the different years you visited. Let's talk about those, all of them."

"OK…" Disney takes a deep breath, "My children would be older than I was when I died. How would any of us deal with that?"

"Would you love them any less because they are older?"

"No, of course not!"

"Then why do you presume to think they would love you less because you may have changed?"

Disney is silent, considering, then slowly nods his head in acceptance.

Steve Jobs enters, wearing more customary heavenly attire—a flowing robe, bespeaking a counselor or learned authority. He slips in silently behind Gabriel. He obviously feels more comfortable and has adjusted to this new way of life. He watches and listens, intrigued

Then Disney asks, "What if the people running my company have made decisions I don't approve of when I return? Do I have any right to change things?"

"You are being given another chance at life with the full knowledge and support of the people in charge of your company," Gabriel explains. "And, as we speak, the best legal minds in the world are working on your rights."

Disney is clearly agitated at the thought, "My rights! I hadn't even thought about the legalities involved. My Social Security number would be inactive. I'm legally dead. Oh, good grief Charlie Brown! How would I take care of myself?"

He leans back on the sill below the viewing window, as the screen focuses on the medical teams working ardently to revive a man they adore.

"Mister Disney," Eepia addresses him, "These people you see are not just working on an experiment. Look at the pink colors around them. They love you. This is personal to every one of them. They actually want you back; not just because this would be a first on so many levels."

He feels weak, "How would I live? I have no rights anymore."

Clemens drags to his feet from the addictively comfortable floating cushion and interjects, "I bullheadedly published a book about General Grant because of my respect for the man. My publishing house went into bankruptcy."

He draws close to Walt's side, "I quite literally had no money at all. I had been advised to settle outright with the people but decided I owed them the full amount. I set out on a speaking tour. Right from the beginning, I was confident with all of my heart that it was an impossible feat. I did it, though. I spoke in countries that did not speak English. I talked in temples. I talked to anyone who would hear me or laugh at my hair. And behold, it worked!"

"What is the moral of that story, Sam, do you know?"

Clemens is absorbed in his memories but sees that Disney is waiting and clears his throat, "You will never have to wait for money. If that's what scares you, forget it. You are the first well-known personage to be brought back to life. People will pay a pretty penny to hear you breathe. And for an autographed picture, even more so."

"That's another thing," Disney says urgently, growing more distressed by the second, "What if I don't have all my past abilities and can achieve just a small portion of my prior life?"

Gabriel shrugs, "I don't have the answer … it is worth considering. Even where we are, there are no guarantees."

Disney stares blankly at the scenes in the lab unfolding before him—the viewing angle focuses wherever Walt is concentrating. He sees the edge of the operating table and the feet of his still-frozen body at the center of the feverishly working medical team's attention.

One flat line registers soundlessly on various monitors.

Suddenly it all changes.…

∞

CHAPTER 23

Back and Forth

DISNEY, Clemens, Eepia, Gabriel, and even Steve Jobs show up as ethereal shimmering spirits in the sterile cryonics operating room, visible only to each other. The slightest energy displacement from their sudden appearance moves the air nearby, but no one on the medical team notices them standing witness—that would create too much havoc for anyone to see.

Staring at the array of machines, Disney asks, "Sam, do you remember those computers we looked at just a while back? What if our minds are like those? What happens once it has been shut off, unplugged? Does it lose its programming'? What if the brain doesn't function? What if I am not the same person when I wake up?"

Clemens jumps in, "Walt, my boy, I remember a statement from another old codger of like mind, Oscar Wilde; iffen I'm correct; he wrote, 'just be yerself, everyone else is already taken'."

Eepia looks tenderly into Disney's eyes, "You will always be you, Mr. Disney, no matter the outcome."

"That is not an absolute," Disney protests. "People suffer memory losses all the time, and they are not dead." He feels helpless, "I cannot fathom the reality that I have been housed in essentially an interred body, hooked up like the puppet Pinocchio waiting for Gepetto to activate him."

Clemens shifts uncomfortably. "I'd like to take this time to thank you for cheering us up—but I can't. Remember how you felt bad about not being able to express your thoughts when you died? Well, you can relax. You've more than made up for it."

"I'm sorry, Sam," Disney is dismayed, "but I need to vent this, and to whom could I turn, if not to you?"

"I understand, but that doesn't mean listening to your thoughts and comments about unburdening yourself before either staying or going brings me solace or consolation. I've watched you feeling sad on a few occasions …

and I've humbly offered comfort and listened to yer past fears without bein' sucked down by them." He points skyward, "I've had much more time up yonder than you, and I've even felt the same once or twice."

"It's good to know you understand my predicament," Walt acknowledges. "I need to know if they would keep me alive today only as a scientific oddity. Could I possibly hope to make more strides in this new age of heart transplants, space travel, microwave ovens, and computers, or do I belong only to the past?"

"No Walt," Gabriel insists, profound respect in his voice, "you were ahead of your time by light-years."

"If I may interpose, Mr. Disney, yes, you were ahead of your day by light-years, pixelating Buzz Light-years." Jobs chuckles at his Pixar reference, "but no one in this group could possibly know about that."

Disney smiles at both Jobs' and Gabriel's assertions. "I appreciate this support. It's just that I'm feeling so overwhelmed. I am not sure I have the nerve to try again, not yet. Gabriel, what if … err, can I try again later maybe?"

Gabriel swiftly waves his hands and arms in response and surrounds them with a sparkling array of colors—their presence still unnoticed by the medical personnel working diligently on the lifeless body before them.

....

They materialize together in Gabriel's plush office in the blink of an eye, and all shake their heads, inquiring in unison, "Gabriel, how did you manage that piece of magic?"

The viewing window behind the desk now shows scenes of various intradimensional images that resemble the photographs sent from by the Hubble telescope.

"Walt, it's your decision; that's why we are here in my office." Gabriel asks, "Anything else?"

"Yes. Did I really make any difference?" Disney is adamant. "I must know for certain before making my choice."

Gabriel glides swiftly behind his desk, searches, then finds an object inside a desk drawer. He holds out a handheld globe, "Walt, look specifically at the two dots in the United States."

"Yes, OK, so what?"

"Oh goody," Eepia declares, "connect the dots, I love playing that."

Gabriel chuckles, "Watch carefully." He presses on both dots. They connect with one another and four other dots appear in other areas. Activated, the dots spread across the globe, each becoming a vibrating golden center. "Each dot represents a theme park sparked by your Imagineering."

Disney looks carefully, intrigued by the other position. "Paris, Japan, and oh my, China?"

As they watch, other multicolored dots appear and burgeon until they encompass the entire globe. "Walt," Gabriel is ecstatic, "see and know: the other colors represent your influence on the hospitality industry, including vacation resorts and a cruise ship or two." He is deeply pleased to produce this visual demonstration. "Now watch carefully."

The globe shoots a fusillade of dots outward to form a pair of vibrating, shimmering, diamond-encrusted mouse ears, and they hear a particularly familiar musical phrase, 'It's a small, small world.'

Disney, overwhelmed, transfixed by the realization dawning on him, but the huge lump in his throat keeps him silent. His eyes are a dead giveaway, however—especially because large tears cascade in streams down his ever-cherubic face.

"You've given many millions, even billions of people all over this world a place where they, too, can suspend their disbelief." Gabriel assures him, "You have definitely made a gigantic difference."

Walt muses, "Being the head of Heaven's Creative Department has been a thrilling and exciting adventure in consciousness and my emotional growth. At first I did not realize that I was not at all suited for the position. Rather than resting on my laurels, or believing that all there was to it was ... just to play and relax in the cloudy structures of my own thinking, I allowed myself to be inspired by the possibilities inherent in the assignment. I am deeply grateful the Powers That Be had the foresight to entrust me with this task. From the blessed viewpoint I've enjoyed during these last five decades, I have seen that the Earth is always under construction and vibrates according to each human's consciousness—evidence of simple cause and effect. Our reality responds to what we think, say, and do, both individually and collectively.

"In Heaven, I quickly found out *I* was in charge of my thoughts—and thoughts become things that come and go according to my intent.

"A Power, a purpose, and an energy permeate in, through, and around all creation—even the atmosphere we breathe has and is a life force. Everyone living on the Earth can experience an ongoing alliance with their individualized life lessons prior to landing—or being born—by accessing free will and free choice, and rejoicing with Love.

"From what I've seen during these extraordinary travels through time with Sam and Eepia, humanity is beginning to realize that earthly upheavals and downswings act like the various tidal flows and waves of the waters of the globe, responding to a power greater than the sum of us. It reminds me of what Swami Vivekenanda said, 'As different streams having different sources all mingle their waters in the sea, so different tendencies, various though they appear, crooked or straight, all lead to God.' Deciding what to see and with whom to interact were predominantly my own choices, whether directed by conscious volition, or needful from a higher authority's perspective.

"I am humbled to recognize how the human spirit is present, readily available, and predisposed to reside within the mind of each person. The body is a vehicle through which the mind operates that can be battered by circumstance until each person realizes he has a mission to accomplish greater than his narrow reality. I see that sometimes it takes more than one lifetime to do what is needed before moving on to higher and higher octaves of aliveness.

"I have been granted the choice to return to earthly life or not: that is the crux of my dilemma. Do I return, now that I've seen so much with my mentor, Sam, and ingénue Eepia? Or shall I remain where I have grown accustomed? A very cushy position, I may add," Walt snickers quietly at his little play on words, "especially for the seat of my own expectations."

Sam and Gabriel are quiet at first, mesmerized by Walt's deeply considered and well articulated thoughts.

Eepia pipes up, "So beautiful and well put, Mr. Disney. I am honored that you are my first mentor."

Surprised to be ignored, Clemens quips to Eepia, "So what am I, chopped liver?"

Pertinent meanings inherent in Walt's soliloquy dawn on each one differently.

Eepia is first to inquire, "About the 'seat of your expectations,' what do you mean? Is that another idiom, or a witticism?"

Gabriel comments, "Walt, it's obvious you have learned a thing or two during the allotted time touring Earth's history—influenced both by your consciousness and a higher power." He glances at Clemens' down-trodden demeanor and encourages, "Yes, Sam, you have earned a merit or two, overshadowing your previous deficiencies, ."

Clemens perks up and smiles, "I've said it before, 'Life is short, break the rules. Forgive quickly, kiss slowly. Love truly. Laugh uncontrollably. And never regret *anything* that makes you smile'."

He speaks warmly to Walt, "so there's nothing to forgive you for. Thank you for letting me go on this li'l excursion of yours." Shaking his head, he adds, "and I'll never forget that consarned song when we went through that ride you called a small, small world. It *did* make me smile, once I got over the shock."

∞

CHAPTER 24

Intervention

BACK at the cryonics lab, the monitors show a continuous flatline—no visible or audible signs of any life, breath, or activity. The team members have stubbornly worked long hours—as long as they dared—to bring Disney back, but despondently, one by one, they make their way out of the sterile room.

An older attending physician, still wearing green scrubs, re-enters and stands, weeping, next to the sheet-draped body. Tears suffusing her voice, she speaks directly to Disney's still lifeless body, "Every person in here felt like you were their very own special friend. Each of us has a memory of Disneyland, Mickey Mouse, Donald Duck, Goofy, Pluto, or a cherished something that makes us feel we owned a little piece of the Magic Kingdom all for ourselves." She grips the rail of the medical bed and cries so hard she is momentarily unable to continue. She sniffs, then wipes her eyes, struggling to regain her professional composure.

....

Clemens looks at Disney and scolds, "Now see what you went and did! And me flat out of candy bars." He adds the inevitable quip, "If you love someone set them free, if you hate someone, set them free, too. Basically, set everyone in your life free and get a dog—people are stupid. Oh, the infirmities of man."

Disney is taken aback by the physician's desperate sadness and wonders aloud, "I didn't realize.... But this doctor, why in Heaven's name would she care?"

As if answering his question, the woman wipes her eyes repeatedly and speaks again. "You made an eye-exercise machine for one of your children with a double-vision problem, administered by Dr. Musgrave in Turlock, California. Someone, somehow, made arrangements for me to use it, too. Within months, my eyes began to work as a unit for the first time since my birth, and they still function as a cohesive system today. I needed to tell

157

you! I want you to understand just how much your generosity meant to Dr. Musgrave and to so many more of us! Without you, we would have remained feeling helpless and unworthy of a good pair of eyes to see properly."

Eepia wipes her eyes in sympathy, deeply touched by this revelation. Clemens fights a lump in his throat.

Still able to counsel Disney, Gabriel gently observes, "You could still do an enormous amount of good, especially with today's advanced technology."

Disney is utterly still. He stares at his inert body, listening.

....

In a far corner of the room, behind a baseboard grate over an air intake filter, the view partially obscured by several unused machines, two set of eyes raptly watch the scene unfold.

Tiny, high-pitched squeaks reveal their owners' presence. "Are you kidding me?" one pipes up urgently, "What are they doing now?"

"Silly mouse, I don't know, I have only one set of eyes just like you; besides, we're down here behind this metal grate. If you want to know more, then get closer. As for me, I'm staying here out of sight."

"Well! OK then, if that's the way you feel, I'll just go by myself. You can view whatever happens from here, but I intend to be in the mix, on the front line, where all the action is."

"Just like always, you seem so full of yourself, just like our maker was … at least that's what I think I heard … I don't remember exactly when. Was it from a distant time, long ago and far away from here? Oh me oh my! I can't recall, my memory's fading. I don't want to lose what I've learned over the years. What can I do?"

"First of all, you can stop whimpering like you usually do, Minnie."

"Me? And you're such a saint! I do remember Walt telling me about how you acted when you were simply Steamboat Willie, right after we had our first conversation about you."

"If you're so smart, when was that?"

"1928 to be precise. And the very next year your name changed to the one we all know, Mickey."

"Well then, I'd say your memory is holding up remarkably well for someone who has been around since …?"

"Hush now!" she interrupts, "we never discuss a lady's age, or have you lost your sense of decency?"

"Guess I'd better get out there before I blow my image after 87 years; gotta keep myself fit and all."

"Mickey, be careful; you're all I've got and if Walt doesn't pull through, I don't know what will become of us."

"I promise. I'll be as quiet as a church mouse. Be back soon." Just under his breath, he adds, "I hope." The famous little rodent with big ears squeezes through the grate, formulating an idea about a vantage point that offers a proper view of any further activities.

CHAPTER *25*

Deciding Moments?

DR. Plaster's tears have subsided, but her emotions are still intense, "Because of that machine, Mr. Disney, people—kids—stopped laughing at my crossed eyes. Can you even imagine how that helped me? For the first time, I gained the confidence to feel good about myself. Life seemed very intimidating and scary when I was a little girl in Livingston. I could easily relate to Bambi on the ice, I was just as awed and fragile."

She dries her face with a tissue, "After Dr. Musgrave shared the machine and I was able to gain control over what appeared to be an impossible problem, nothing ever frightened me that much again."

She glances around to check the several monitors, still hoping to see or hear some signs of physical life. "My personal confidence and determination never allow me to accept barriers—I look only for possibilities. And to tell you a secret, my theme song has always been "When You Wish Upon a Star."

. . . .

Hearing these heartfelt confidences, Disney's eyes fill with renewed tears. Gabriel pats him on the shoulder.

Still the innocent, Eepia wonders aloud, "How could anyone not be her friend?"

The good doctor continues, "When I heard you had passed all the preliminary tests before being revived, I pulled rank with an on-call doctor to let me attend to you."

She dabs her shining eyes and smiles at Disney's body before her, "We are a team, you and I, whether you know it or not. When I was a teenager I created a dear little cartoon character I called 'Boo-Boo.' After high school, I got a scholarship and parlayed my cartooning talents into a work-type program for an agency that was a competitor of yours, but I didn't care. I had other goals. When I learned about your health deteriorating because of cancer and your impending cryonic suspension, I thought about what you had done for me and for others without regard for rewards and accolades and, well, I wanted to give back because of the generosity you'd modeled. You had given from your heart. Dr. Musgrave was very thankful too for all you'd done."

She gently re-examines the dormant body, looking for even minute, telltale life signs. Finding none, her shoulders droop slightly, but ever the professional she documents her findings on the clipboard at the foot of the bed. "The people I had been cartooning for offered to buy me out and I leapt at the chance, because that would fund my medical training. I leveraged my artistic talent and became a medical illustrator. I was determined to learn more about the physical body, anatomy, bone structures, and everything involved, beyond anything I'd read so far. With several tutors' help, I challenged a few college entrance exams."

She pauses to take a breath and exhales, "Anyway, I was granted provisional admission to one school as a trial and I jumped at the chance. I chose to learn about geriatrics, which became my specialty. It took me longer than most other students to complete all the necessary training, but since then I've never stopped learning, or challenging myself. I still dabble with cartooning: I doodle a few happy-faced flowers on sheets of stationery from time to time, mainly when my mind is freewheeling. It helps me concentrate more fully on what's at stake."

She holds up the clipboard and points to the patient history, wishing and hoping Disney might open his eyes. "See?" The body is still, and Dr. Plaster sadly reattaches the clipboard to the foot of the bed. The rubbing metal squeaks.

....

"What was that? Minnie, did you hear anything?" Mickey has made it to the top of a light fixture above the bed that gave him a clearer view of the man on the table and the woman pacing almost constantly around him. Mickey edges closer to the side, hoping to peer over.

The other mouse shakes her head no. "Don't you get too close now, dear, you know your balance is not the same as it once was."

....

"I care for you," Dr. Plaster continues, "more than you'll ever know. My dream—which you helped make possible—is to help bring about changes in science. That idea has pulled me forward for more years than I care to count."

A bank of overhead lights flickers unexpectedly, then resumes steady illumination. The doctor shifts her attention toward the disturbance and an odd shadow wobbles momentarily on the ceiling.

She glances up, then looks back at Disney as she continues to explain, "Before I retire, my all-consuming wish is to see you again—alive, robust, healthy—no matter how long it takes. But…" she coughs, betraying a deeper condition, "my health is fading, as is my eyesight, or insight as I'd like to think of it. It's time for you to come back without delay. Let's make a pact: I'll trade places with you, how about that?"

She is shocked at her sudden revelatory notion. She considers the illogic of her suggestion and says, "No matter … conditions have changed since they first suspended you back in '66. Imagine that! Your particular ailment has been declared manageable, and the medical community deems some forms are even curable."

Dr. Plaster frowns dramatically, "If you hadn't smoked, you might have lived a healthy and even fuller, more productive life, longer than your first 66-year tour. I know this for certain: today's world needs you."

She wipes her teary eyes and admits her deeper truth, "I need you!"

Witness to these powerful, personal confidences, Disney is nearly speechless. "How could I still have an impact after these decades of being technically dead?"

"Who in holy tarnation cares?" Clemens moans, "You're not only a consarned puddin'-headed dunderhead if you make her cry any longer, you are but a coward."

Dr. Plaster crumples onto the edge of the bed next to Disney's motionless, lifeless body, and sobs uncontrollably.

Clemens is adamant, "You have a chance to walk right back into life and make some remarkable strides. Instead of looking at the possibilities, you are concentrating on the missing hole in the doughnut. Enjoy the pastry you have been gifted with, my friend. If that morsel were given to me, that opportunity handed to me, I'd be terrified, but I'd jump at it. You have that adventurous spirit, too. Why aren't you chomping at the bit? Go on back."

Eepia thoughtfully addresses Disney, "I will miss you, but we will talk again, and I will hear about your special moments. And I will envy you. I would go for you if I could."

Gabriel interjects, "Please, friends! Walt must make this decision alone. If he sees no merit in returning to his body, it is his choice. We must say no more."

Eepia whispers in Disney's ear, "That lady needs you. Her color is fading, turning dark."

Clemens also whispers in Disney's other ear, "I once said, 'the two most important days in your life are the day you are born and the day you find out why.' It takes some of us a bit longer to find out the why. You, my longtime friend, are a potential miracle in progress. The world needs Walt Disney. I will miss you … and I expect a full accounting upon your return."

Disney turns to those surrounding him, smiling "A man has never been more blessed with good friends. Thank you, each of you." He tentatively reaches out and gently touches his body, then immediately pulls away.

"Thank you, Sam, my mentor and benign agitator, you are so much more than a prognosticator. Are you some kind of wizard?"

"No, that title was given to Thomas Edison, in Menlo Park, New Jersey, I believe; may he continue to rest in peace."

Disney pauses, "For telling me what I oughta do and by doing my thinking for me, that's just what I needed…. I've made up my mind."

Gabriel eagerly asks, "And pray tell what is it?" He wants to know the result without the reasons, but quickly realizes his mistake and acquiesces, "Walt, please go ahead."

Disney nods, "It's like this: the Berlin Wall held sway until it was time for it to come down. Through history, the times we were under attack by other people consumed either by fear or the need to control are truly discomforting. That youngster in China stood his ground for what he believed in. The weather has been wild and we've weathered those storms. I've been distressed by the indifference in some people and watched them change from helplessness to helpfulness, regardless of location or circumstances.

"All of this amounts to seeing life on Earth with new eyes, and oh my, when I saw all those dots on Gabriel's globe showing that what I created has multiplied manyfold … the ripples literally surround the planet."

He pauses to catch his breath, "I saw the inherent goodness that supersedes the darker parts of humanity, even in my beloved Magic Kingdoms. Therefore, I am confident that what my thoughts placed before me, misguided later, was out of my hands entirely. I thought they were mistakes, but they ultimately helped me to realize the truth: humankind is growing through its ever-expanding group consciousness. And when someone or some government body overtly becomes self-aggrandizing, more people will eventually see the error of their ways, stand up, and take back what's inherently theirs in the first place… a form of self-government. For this I am grateful."

Sam is anxious to break his silence with another of his usual rants, "And… about those rapscallions… I remember when…"

"Enough pontificating, Sam," Gabriel interrupts, "let Walt finish. Time is of the essence, or haven't you noticed?"

"We've all weathered so many storms in our time." Disney continues, "Disasters happen; however they're made, created by nature or humankind itself. What it means to me now is this: change is inevitable, how we respond to it is optional. We can learn or not; we can choose to hide our heads in the proverbial sand, or rise to the situation and work to find solutions. Ultimately, it doesn't matter what label it bears, whether the event is "right" or not; it's neither, it simply is."

He looks at his still lifeless body, then steadily at Clemens, Gabriel, Eepia, and Jobs in turn.

"Being self-absorbed is not the way for humanity to grow and prosper. Each of us must teach another, somehow. The pace at which technology has evolved is far beyond anything I could have dreamed up, yielding advances both exceptional and ordinary. Technology itself is only as good as the one using it."

Disney looks at the attending physician, recognizes she is indeed the same little girl from Livingston he had watched from heaven, now all grown up. "I apologize for being a tyrant in my day. I gave rein to my darker side far too many times, and since then I've done my best by heading up Heaven's Creative Department to lead the way and inspire others to follow by being a better example. I recall what Gandhi said: be the person you want to see in this world."

Eepia agrees enthusiastically, "And by being that person, the world is changed one person at a time. At some given point, enough of us change-lings will tip the scales and the earth will bask in a new awareness and consciousness."

Clemens replies, "I must remark, Eepia, how articulate you've become. I'm glad to have been an example and a mentor of sorts."

"An example of both sides of the behavioral aisle, yes." Gabriel grins and winks at Eepia. "Sam, meritoriously speaking, you have done well; another positive mark may be in the offing sometime soon if you continue in this vein."

Gabriel realizes he wants to know—needs to know—an answer, "Walt, why did you decide to write the name, 'Kurt Russell' on a piece of paper right before you left the earth plane? You've never once discussed that these past fifty years. Why is that?"

"All in all," Disney shrugs and admits, "I think it's best to let that sleeping dog lie." He looks over at his lifeless body, "This one too."

Gabriel realizes what the original Imagineer has just announced and points upward, inquiring, "Going my way?" He stretches out his arms to gather them closer.

An elevator magically appears, the doors open, and they step in—except Disney. Gabriel holds the doors open.

Disney looks back at his body and says fondly, "Goodbye my friend. It's time for all of us to move along. I've held on to you long enough."

The elevator door closes and dematerializes as it ascends.

Dr. Plaster has been looking intently at her patient, and now does a double take—a smile of contentment somehow has appeared on his face!

∞

CHAPTER 26

You Can't Take it With You

*A*S 87-year-old Mickey Mouse leans farther over the lip of the light fixture to peek at Disney's body, he feels his delicate balance on the lighting bank shift suddenly. It sways slightly at first, then swings back and forth and gains momentum until he loses his balance and tumbles downward. Horrified, he yells a warning that comes out as little high-pitched squeaks: "Ohhhhh, nooo! Here I come, ready or not! Look out below!"

The mouse disrupts the entire sterile scene and lands squarely on Disney's chest. He sees several ethereal forms heading into a shimmering elevator, but quickly scampers down along the body and legs, striving to make a fast, uncomplicated getaway without being noticed.

A monitor loudly beeps once, twice, three times, showing an irregular heartbeat, and the screen shows intermittent spikes on the heart monitor, but then resumes a flat line.

Dr. Plaster slowly looks up in bewilderment, furiously blinks back the tears in her eyes and stares in complete horror at the famous mouse scurrying across Walt Disney's body. Abruptly, it jumps on to her.

She glares at Mickey, astonished, totally dumbfounded, and faints at the shock. She slumps onto the hard floor.

Now, don't that beat all. (We can hear Sam Clemens' comment as if he were still in the room.) *Upstaged by a rodent with big ears.*

THE END

∞

Truth or Fiction?

Author Wayne Edmiston's notes about book details and facts about people, places, and experiences:

Chapter 1: To learn more about cryonic suspension, please visit this site: www.alcor.org/FAQs/index.html.

Chapter 2: Dr. Musgrave, from Turlock, California, and what happened with the little girl is true; told to me by the one who was there, Sherry (my late wife).

Chapter 3: Mitchell's Ice Cream Parlor is still there. The minor incident was reported the next day in the San Francisco Chronicle, Friday, March 22, 1968. "President's daughter, Lynda Bird Johnson, ordered off cable car for eating ice cream cone."

Chapter 4: University of California at Berkeley and its Vietnam War-era upheavals were real. Samuel Clemens' papers are indeed housed in the Bancroft Library at UC Berkeley.

Chapter 5: Not of this Earth, 1969. The first Lunar landing with astronauts Armstrong and Aldrin was indeed accurate. What happened after they left the moon's surface is the authors' imagination and speculation.

Chapter 6: Political activist Joan Baez did play at Woodstock, sang the last two songs mentioned in the text, and gave birth to a son she named Gabriel. Any dialog among our three characters is again comes from pure imagination.

The first episode of Mr. Roger's Neighborhood aired on NBC during that time.

Chapter 7: Warner Studios, Los Angeles, California, mid-1973. Specifically, the set of the Bonanza television series. Episode #422 is correct; but what happened on set during the filming is pure conjecture. The actors named therein are also a matter of record, and the sudden passing of beloved

169

Dan Blocker (Hoss) is sadly accurate. Victor Sen Yung, the actor who played Hop Sing, mentioned the incident on set during a television interview. A real event not included in this book, may have saved his life; Yung said he saw the spirit of Hoss just before boarding an airplane flight and did not travel. The plane crashed, killing many.

Chapter 8: Menlo Park, CA, is where Steve Jobs, Steve Wozniak, and Ron Wayne worked in their garage, perfecting their first personal computer, and founded Apple. The recorded meeting is, of course, drawn from my imagination. The story in which Clemens talks about 'unconscious plagiarism' is in one of his many books, synthesized to fit in this narrative. Apple was founded on April Fools' Day, 1976.

Chapter 9: The bank heist is completely fictional.

Chapter 10: The Los Angeles Olympics took place 1984; the exchanges with the runner and biker(s) are entirely imaginary.

Chapter 11: EPCOT Center. Michael Jackson was in fact there. The Captain EO show first launched at Epcot, and the song, "Man in the Mirror," became a mega hit. The inventors of 3-D are correctly identified as Edwin Porter and William Waddell.

Chapter 12: A figment of my imagination.

Chapter 13: Kathryn Sullivan and Orson Scott Card are real peopl, and what Gabriel said about their potential future is true and correct. What happened to and with them in this book, however, was born of my imagination.

Chapter 14: October 19, 1987, New York City. Black Monday did happen that day, as recounted in history books. Their experiences in the apartment, however, is imaginary.

Chapter 15: Tiananmen Square protests turned into a horrendous massacre between April 15, 1989 and June 4, 1989. It took a full two days to haul away the dead bodies that had been discarded like trash in the streets, adding to the already rotting trash that had piled up. Reports aver the stench was unimaginable. The injured were turned away from the hospitals because the government refused them aid; China's First Emperor, Qin, and his entombed Terra Cotta army are factual; but the accounting of what happened to the young man with the Mylar balloon has been altered to fit the scenario.

Chapter 16: Berlin, Germany. President Kennedy's speech took place at the Brandenburg Gate, recorded in 1963. The Wall fell apart because of the thousands of people hammering and chiseling on November 9, 1989. What the photographer captured and Eepia's watery experience are pure conjecture.

Chapter 17: All tragically true: September 11, 2001, New York City and the Twin Towers of the World Trade Center; the second space shuttle accident; Phuket, Thailand, December 26, 2004, 9:45 a.m., Boxing Day, tsunami.

Chapter 18: Disneyworld and Disneyland 2005 attractions are true; Disney's reminiscences about his childhood in Missouri are documented. Jingles was Disney's favorite carousel horse. The RESERVED sign and experience with the unruly child are imaginary fancies.

Chapter 19: The French Quarter of New Orleans, 2005, Hurricane Katrina is historical truth; what our travelers encountered is strictly conjecture and from my imagination.

Chapters 20 to 24 are all products of my imagination.

Chapter 25: Sherry's self-disclosure about creating the cartoon character, BooBoo, is true. The rest of the chapter is fiction.

Chapter 26: The names of the mice are from Walt Disney himself. What they went through came straight from *my* imagination.

∞

About the Author

WAYNE EDMISTON is a fourth-generation Californian, a fifth-generation teacher, and an Eagle Scout. He served in the Air Force for almost four years, including an 11-month tour in Vietnam (1969) as a crew chief for an RF-101 Voodoo aircraft, and honorably discharged as a Staff Sergeant; Life Member of the Veterans of Foreign Wars, (VFW.)

He earned his bachelor's degree and a California State teaching life credential at Chico State College. Throughout his teaching career, Edmiston focused on special education.

He taught both academic and vocational subjects in four of California State's correctional institutions. As a correctional educator for 21 years, he wore many hats, including acting academic supervisor, senior librarian, literacy coordinator for GED and college distant learning programs, chief

GED examiner, and assistant literacy supervising Laubach tutor–trainer, and was a member of the State Planning Panel for Corrections with California Literacy for five years. He spent two more years as the community living skills facilitator for the state mental hospital at Atascadero.

Both he and his wife, Jacque, are ordained New Thought ministers with Centers for Spiritual Living and teach Science of Mind principles. They are nondenominational wedding officiants and respect all couples, including LGBTQ families and prison inmates.

Their website is **OneSpiritBeachWeddings.com**.

As a writer and author, the screenplay version of his family-oriented, science fiction story, *Unfatally Dead: to Thaw or Not to Thaw?* was a finalist in two contests. Both the play and the subsequent ebook depict a fascinating time-traveling journey of two icons, Samuel Clemens (known worldwide as Mark Twain), and Walt Disney, accompanied by Eepia, a new soul. Wayne has also written a children's book, *Ellie and Her Elephant,* and is working on a three-part "thrillology" drawn from personal metaphysical experiences he has fictionalized to protect some of the characters, living or not.

Other written works are in progress.

Edmiston is involved with reader's theatre at the South County Historical Society in San Luis Obispo County. He and Jacque reside on California's Central Coast with their Lhasa Apso mix dog, Sophie.

Find Wayne on the web at www.**wedmiston.com.**

∞

ELLIE &
HER ELEPHANT

Ellie and her Elephant is about a young physically challenged girl, Ellie, who enters a contest to name a soon-to-be-born baby elephant at the local zoo. She sends in her own name as her entry, because the local mayor ruled that the name must begin with an E and the second letter be an L. Wearing a blindfold, the mayor draws the winning name: Ellie! Our young heroine is honored to have named the baby elephant and takes the added responsibilities seriously. Years later, we learn that elephants truly do *not* forget.

Ellie's father, a music store owner in their small California town, weaves a beautiful, entertaining tale for Ellie's friends about how music came into being, as well as fun facts about the piano, his favorite instrument. The story inspires Ellie—she had not been excited about learning to play *any* instrument, but when her fingers touch the black-and-white keys for the first time, **magic happens**!

She grows up playing the piano every chance she gets. Eventually, Ellie earns a partial music scholarship that includes housing for students with physical limitations. Coincidentally, her father had attended the same community college years before.

Ellie finds love in the eyes of her physical therapist. His love and encouragement help her reach her secret goals to gain strength and walk— for the first time—to surprise her father on her graduation day.

Along with the story, Wayne has included several thinking questions for young readers to answer, whether just in their own minds, or by writing their thoughts in spaces on the pages. Children can learn great principles through their own personal inquiry by engaging with the book. (That is so much better than preaching!) When an individual experiences and decides for him- or herself, rather than when he or she is told, learning happens.

Also by Wayne Edmiston

Diary of the Three Savants: The Beginning

A prequel, *The Beginning* sets the scene for an upcoming sci-fi tale. When three siblings—Alan, Alice, and Andrew—finally reunite many years after they were cruelly forced apart, suddenly their lives feel complete again. They spent many years in separate mental institutions but, restored to each other, the trio quickly sets to work and embarks on a journey aimed at preserving the future of Earth for generations to come. Along the way, their paths cross with Alvin T. Dogg, whose car has broken down for reasons he cannot quite comprehend, and Alan, Alice, and Andrew know they must act *now*, without a moment to lose.

In this book, Wayne Edmiston fully prepares us for a sure-to-be riveting upcoming tale about four lives that intersect to save the human race. We learn about Alvin T. Dogg's life both before and after meeting the trio, and we see the vast contrast between the underdog he was and his swift transformation into the overachiever he becomes before our eyes. Alvin's anger, frustration, and disbelief about what befalls him, combined with the three siblings' "higher beings" status, has left this reviewer salivating for more. The characters' exciting adventure meets our deepest expectations, and I am sure you'll join me in anxiously awaiting the release of their continuing exploits, set in a time and place long forgotten and out of this world. I very much enjoyed reading *Diary of the Three Savants: The Beginning* and wholeheartedly recommend it to science fiction fans.

– Rosie Malezer for Readers' Favorite

Also by Wayne Edmiston

Crisis at Paradise Eye-Land

Join the lusty protagonist on a journey that involves an unexpected combination: seedy strip joints and the parwanormal. Lynden Rykker runs an adult strip club, Paradise Eye-Land in California and, after five years, she yearns for a new challenge in her life. But strange, unexplained things are happening in the club, and the apparent aim seems to be eliminating the club altogether. Elsewhere, we learn about an interior designer, Jenny, who is about to experience the full force of an entity called Mike Lee, as he savagely takes over her mind and body. What happens to Jenny and those she meets will have deadly results. Can anyone help her regain control of her body from the evil and vengeful Lee?

If you enjoy a story that has twists, turns, and surprises throughout, *Crisis at Paradise Eye-Land* is a perfect book for you. The writer has woven amazing detail into his characters and story lines. Each character is well constructed and their dialogue is perfect. Wayne Edmiston has built scenes that are so realistic they touch every one of your senses. A superb story from start to finish.

I loved the part of the story when Jenny was trying to reclaim her physical body from Lee; the tension was terrific. The ending—in fact, the entire story—was not what I expected. Just when I thought I knew what was going to happen, the author took me in another direction. A perfect and unique story, and excellently executed!

– Lesley Jones for Readers' Favorite

WEDMISTON

PUBLISHING

www.ingramcontent.com/pod-product-compliance
Lightning Source LLC
Chambersburg PA
CBHW021019120726
47905CB00009B/3080